Where Were You

Nicholas E

First published by Robert Hale Limited in 1981

Copyright © Nicholas Best 1981

This edition published in 2021 by Lume Books
30 Great Guildford Street,
Borough, SE1 0HS

The right of Nicholas Best to be identified as the author of this work has been asserted by them in accordance with the Copyright, Design and Patents Act, 1988.

All rights reserved. No part of this publication may be reproduced, stored in a retrieval system, or transmitted in photocopying, recording or otherwise, without the prior permission of the copyright owner.

Table of Contents

Author's Note	5
1	7
2	14
3	23
4	35
5	47
6	63
7	75
8	83
9	98
10	102
11	114
12	123
13	135
14	146
15	158
16	176

Author's Note

Any similarity between *Where Were You At Waterloo?* and real events is entirely the fault of the real events, which took place either immediately before publication or just afterwards

1

About five a.m. on the morning of the Queen's official birthday parade, Guardsman Turtle of Her Majesty's Gobelin Guards slipped quietly out of bed and tiptoed into the washroom to give his bearskin a shampoo. While the rest of 9 Platoon were still asleep in the barrack block, Turtle dunked his head-dress in a basin of hot water and squirted Vosene suds over it until he had worked up a fine lather. He sang a little song to himself as he did so. Today's parade, known to the ignorant as Trooping the Colour, was important to Turtle. It would be the first time that he and his Sovereign had worked together professionally. He wanted her to catch him at his best.

When he had finished shampooing the bearskin, Turtle rinsed it twice under the shower before giving it a brisk pummelling with his green army towel. Then he took it into the boiler room and left it to dry.

By six thirty, he couldn't do a thing with it.

It had dried all right, but it had dried like frightened candy floss. To Turtle, tearfully raking the fur with gobs of brilliantine, it was obvious that his world was about to collapse.

At eight o'clock, Sergeant Ball broke the news to Sebastian Clinch. 'I shall have to get rid of him, sir,' he said. 'There's nothing else for it. I won't have him going on television looking like that. The cameras will pick him up, wherever he stands. They can't miss.'

Nor could they. Seventeen years old and six foot four, thin as a flagpole, Turtle was a conspicuous sight. He was not easily lost in a crowd.

'And another thing,' continued Ball. 'With the battalion going on Spearhead this afternoon, he's got to make out a will. In case he gets shot. He's asked you to witness it, sir. He won't have anyone else. Says it's personal.'

'I'll talk to him after the parade,' said Sebastian.

'If you would sir, please. By 1400 hours. I have to get the wills back to the Company clerk before we go on active service. Otherwise it might be too late.'

The heavy equipment had been packed and weighed, ready for airlift. The light equipment would follow as soon as the birthday parade was over. At two o'clock that afternoon, the 1st Battalion, the Gobelin Guards would go on standby as Spearhead of the British army for the month of June.

The Spearhead commitment lasts thirty days and is shared in rotation between all infantry regiments stationed in the British Isles. It is a commitment to fly anywhere in the world at twenty-four hours' notice. In theory it could mean typhoon relief work in Hong Kong, a peace-keeping role in Cyprus, an anti-Communist presence in the Gulf. In practice, or so it appeared to Sebastian, Spearhead in the post-imperial 1980s meant one place only – Northern Ireland. The Irish were hotting up for their silly season, culminating in the annual Apprentice Boys' march. A month on standby would surely require a trip across the Irish Sea to reinforce the tightly-stretched regular troops, in Derry perhaps or South Armagh. The question was not if, but when.

There were thirty men in 9 Platoon, average age twenty. Each of them had signed an official document that morning, warning them for immediate service overseas. Regular leave had been suspended for a month. Nobody would step outside the barrack gate without leaving a telephone number for contact in an emergency. The smell of action hung sharp and chill in the air. Every soldier in the platoon, every soldier in the battalion, knew that by the same time next week he might be dead.

Sebastian worried about all the men under his command, but about none more than Turtle. The others knew how to look after themselves. Partridge, his orderly, had grown up in a slum. Gilligan, a sombre mercurial Irishman, had volunteered for the battalion's last tour in Belfast. Turtle was different. If anyone in 9 Platoon was daft enough to accept a powdered glass sandwich from a girl whose smile hid IRA sympathies, or follow her twinkling buttocks to a party with a guest list of one, Turtle was. Sebastian feared for his life.

Horse Guards Parade, one minute to eleven. Eight detachments of Foot Guards drawn up to await the arrival of the Queen. The Grenadier Guards at the right of the line, because theirs was the Colour to be trooped today. Next the Gobelin Guards, identified by a yellow plume in the bearskin. Beyond them, elements of the Scots, Irish, Welsh and Coldstream Guards, in that order. Spectators lining the square, ladies in picture hats and gentlemen in morning coats. Chelsea pensioners in dress uniform, wearing their medals; old men and boy scouts standing together. Television cameras relaying the spectacle to twelve million living-rooms. Sunshine, flags and good humour. The nation was gathering to honour its Monarch.

On one side of the square stood the garden wall of 10 Downing Street. On the other, Churchill's war house and the old Admiralty building. The space in between had been used as a tilt yard during the reign of Elizabeth I. Later it became an assembly point for royal troops. Soldiers drilled here before the War of the Spanish Succession. It was here, on a cold morning in February 1793, that George III reviewed the Gobelin Guards before sending them to Holland to open the first campaign of the Napoleonic Wars. The dust was rich beneath Sebastian's feet. The ground had seen men in his uniform depart for the Crimea and the Boer War; it had seen them go twice to France this century to fight the Germans. The history of the Gobelin Guards, more than three hundred years of it, was the history of this ground.

The regiment was raised by King Charles II in 1652 to provide a royal bodyguard. It is the only regiment in the army to owe name and title to the charms of a woman. In 1652 Charles was an exile in Paris, a fugitive from Cromwell's England, hunted and penniless. Mlle de Gobelin (she added 'de' in honour of the royal connection) was a tapestry saleswoman who called on him with a selection of wallhangings and stayed to become his mistress. As a saleswoman she was not a success. She ended up lending Charles 3000 pistoles to finance a company of guards for the protection of his person. Duly and uncharacteristically grateful, he named them in her honour.

Yet the Regiment's tradition goes back much further than 1652. It goes back at least as far as the monarchy, to the house carls of King Harold, defenders of their liege at the Battle of Hastings. Strong blond men who would die rather than give ground to the Norman invaders – and did. A thousand years had gone into the making of the Gobelin Guards, a thousand years of royal soldiering and taut professional pride. Men like Sergeant Ball, his moustache curling into his eyes, fought beside Henry V on St Crispin's Day. Men like Sebastian, too. And men like Turtle. A hastily-borrowed bearskin had restored his equilibrium and he had wiped away his tears; he was on parade in scarlet tunic, at the end of the line furthest from the cameras. In days gone by, the ancestors of Ball and Sebastian and Turtle had known what it was to march to war. In days to come, Sebastian hoped and prayed, so would they.

The clock above the Horse Guards building was nudging eleven. Preceded by an escort of jingling horsemen, the Queen came into view from the direction of Buckingham Palace. She was riding side-saddle and wore the white plume of the Grenadiers in her hat. Behind her, swathed in gold braid, rode Prince Charles and the Duke of Edinburgh. At the first chime of the clock came the order to present arms. 'Royal salute. Present *hipe!*' Sword to lip, Sebastian kissed the hilt and lowered the blade with a swish towards the ground. The audience stood up. Above their heads, the clock struggled gamely for a while, then lapsed into silence as the band began to play.

Suddenly a man broke away from the crowd and vaulted the barriers onto the square. Slipping between two policemen, he headed straight for the Queen. His eyes glittered, and his face was twisted with hate. In his hand, he brandished a revolver.

Sebastian didn't hesitate for a moment. While the rest of the army were still gaping, he sprinted towards the would-be assassin. The crowd gasped. Twelve million viewers rocketed forward on their chairs. The madman saw his danger too late. Even as he raised his weapon to shoot the Queen, Sebastian drove his sword deep into his chest, killing him instantly. Or maybe he chopped off his head – Sebastian could never decide which. Then, covered in blood, he seized hold of the Queen's horse to prevent it bolting.

'Who is that young man?' she asked, after she had got over the shock.
'Lieutenant Sebastian Clinch, Your Majesty.'
'Arise, Sir Sebastian…'

The spirit was willing, but the opportunity stubbornly refused to present itself. No lunatics were waiting for the Queen as she returned from inspecting the ranks. No assassins lurked under the arches of the Horse Guards building. Sebastian's time had not yet come.

Instead the trooping began. With stately tread the red-gold Colour was borne aloft down the line of Guards, so that all might recognise and rally to it in battle. An escort of Grenadiers marched alongside in a protective phalanx. The ceremony had served a real purpose in times past, a symbolic one now. Towards the end of its journey, the Colour passed a few feet in front of Sebastian. It was gripped by a young ensign, lugubrious of face, erect of carriage. His lips trembled in silent incantation above his gleaming curb chain. His right elbow, held parallel to the ground, was burning with cramp.

Out of one eye Sebastian watched him revert to his original position at the right of the line. This was the signal for the remainder of the parade, who had not moved during the troop, to get their legs back. Gratefully the men formed close order for the march past. At the beat of the drum, all eight detachments stepped off together. The Gobelins were in No 3 Guard, officers at the front in line abreast. They were led by the Company commander, Major the Earl of Malplaquet, MVO, *psc*. He was the man to follow. If he put a foot wrong – which was quite possible, even with Sergeant Ball bellowing at him from behind – he would drop everyone in it.

It was very necessary for Sergeant Ball to bellow. The din was terrific. Lord Malplaquet's words of command, more confident than distinct, were snatched away by the noise of the band. Some officers, unsure of their vocal chords, had taken extra lessons from an opera singer in advance of the parade. It had not occurred to Malplaquet to join them.

'Steady, sir! Fill to your left!' Ball was stern, and full of authority, as if restraining a cocker spaniel. Obediently, Malplaquet did as he was told. He could not see what was going on behind him. He knew only that the march past was a complex manoeuvre, easier to conceive than to execute. There were corners to negotiate, and orders to be given on the correct foot at the right moment. No laughing matter when the eyes of millions were upon him. A cock-up, even a small one, could damage his career.

No 3 Guard had hit the home straight now, more or less intact, and there, up ahead, was the Queen. Her face was impassive, but her eyes did not miss a trick. Through a haze of dust the Guardsmen drew nearer and nearer until, at length, they were almost level. This was the moment they had been waiting for. The moment for which the spring months had been spent in rehearsal. The moment the Drill Sergeant – not normally an angry man – had insisted would never come, because the Queen would die laughing long before the exhibition that was No 3 Guard ever reached her.

'No 3 Guard!' yelled Malplaquet. 'Eyees – right!' Seventy pairs of eyeballs rattled in seventy skulls and three swords dipped in homage. The Queen acknowledged with a white-gloved hand. Earnest faces looked her squarely in the eye – Sebastian Clinch, conscious somehow of an unwritten debt to history; Turtle, aware that his mother had taken the day off from the factory to watch on television; Sergeant Ball, determined that nothing should go wrong now. And then the moment was over. The troops had gone past and were staring at the spectators in the stands. There remained only a halt to reform the ranks, a display by the cavalry – all tinsel and glitter – and the ceremony would be complete. Once the Royal Family had been escorted back to Buckingham Palace, the birthday would be out of the way again for another twelve months.

The gates of Chelsea Barracks stood wide to admit the returning troops. Watched through the railings by a handful of curious civilians, the men of No 3 Guard teetered forward on their toes in expectation of the order to dismiss.

It was 12.45. There was just time to change before lunch. In fifteen minutes a fly past of RAF jets from Strike Command would roar over the palace and across central London, the last public tribute of the day. An hour later, in camouflaged combat jackets and rubber boots, the battalion would go on Spearhead, packed, loaded and ready to move. Every man in barracks, six hundred in all, wondered what, if anything, the afternoon would bring.

2

'I'd say it went off okay, sir, considering,' said Partridge, undoing Sebastian's collar with practised fingers.

'Think so? So do I. Mind that top hook, would you.'

'Any road, it's another one you won't have to do again. Which uniform will you be wearing for lunch?'

'The blue jumper. That's easiest. And hurry it up – they're serving champagne in the mess.'

'I know, sir. The Colour Sarnt opened a bottle earlier to make sure it wasn't flat for the officers.'

If he had been drinking champagne at his master's expense, Partridge betrayed no sign of it. He took Sebastian's tunic and dusted it carefully before putting it in the wardrobe. Then he slipped a blue patrol from its hanger and held open the sleeves.

'Any news on Spearhead?' Sebastian asked. As a subaltern he was supposed to hear about Spearhead long before the other ranks, but Partridge's position as an orderly gave him access to many and irregular channels of information denied to junior officers.

'No sir, nothing official. But I think it'll be Derry, all the same. It says in the *Standard* that they was throwing stones there this morning. The Prods was flying union jacks to celebrate the Queen's birthday, and the Catholics didn't like it at all. There's a photo too. The paper reckons they'll need extra troops to control it if it escalates.'

Derry. How did the song go? *I lost my balls at Derry's walls*. Maybe not his balls, thought Sebastian. Maybe he would just get a bullet through the spine and finish up strapped into a wheelchair for the rest of his days, dribbling down his front and being fed with a spoon.

'Derry, eh? You'll enjoy that, won't you, Partridge?'

'Not me, sir. I've only got two hundred and fourteen to do. Then I'm out. I don't want to go back to Ulster if I can help it.'

It was one of the happy fictions of Partridge's life that when his three years in the army were up, he would not rush to sign on again. Both he and Sebastian knew different. Partridge had enlisted for the three Fs – feeding, fighting and fornicating – and knew very well that there was nothing in civilian life to touch it.

Still only nineteen, he was a thickset youth who had joined the Gobelin Guards straight from borstal. He had been sent to borstal for stealing a motor bike, but told his friends it was rape. One of his muscular forearms bore the tattooed legend *For ever – Tracy*, the other *True love – Sharon*. Beneath his shirt, *Mild* was stencilled over the right nipple and *Bitter* over the left. He was engaged to a girl called Christine in Nottingham, but in the meantime was walking out with Dirty Dot, the battalion slag, who waited for him every evening outside the barrack gate. He was not promiscuous so much as confused. As soon as his duties were over for the day, and sometimes before, Partridge the skinhead would change into his bird-trapping outfit – bovver boots and regimental braces – and stride innocently out of the gate under the disapproving eye of the Sergeant-in-Waiting. Once out of sight of the guardroom, he would slip into a doorway and insert the gold earring he always wore off duty, before setting out for an evening of pleasure with Dot. The details of his adventures with Dot, wide-ranging in scope, were always related in full to Sebastian next morning.

Surprisingly, for one so unbridled, Partridge relished the job of soldier-servant. Since most of his duties revolved around Sebastian, he could safely remain inside the officers' mess pantry whenever there were unpleasant tasks to be carried out. He spent much of his day sitting in an armchair with a cigarette dangling from his lips, listening to Radio One and pretending to polish his master's boots. Occasionally he would disappear to the kitchen for an hour or so to have a cup of tea – unless it happened that the kitchen staff had any silver to be cleaned, in which case he would plead urgent officer's business elsewhere and effect a swift withdrawal. He had discovered that a soldier carrying a cloth and hastening intently down the corridor is rarely, if ever, challenged as to the exact nature of his errand.

It was a soft number, and Partridge knew it. It shielded him from innumerable irksome duties – among them, Trooping the Colour – and it carried certain perks as well, such as handing round glasses of port on Dinner Nights in the mess. Partridge usually discharged this task on the basis of one for the officer who had ordered it and one for Partridge. If enough officers ordered port, he would burp and call Sebastian by his Christian name before the evening was out.

But the greatest perk of all, in Partridge's view, was that he was allowed to drive his master's smart blue Mercedes sports car whenever Sebastian was on guard duty and needed fetching. Partridge was enormously proud of this car. In fact, though he couldn't prove it, Sebastian was convinced that a pair of tights he discovered under the seat after being collected from a 48-hour guard at Windsor belonged to the incorrigible Dot. They undoubtedly belonged to someone. Partridge, as a matter of instinct, went all glassy eyed and had no idea how the tights got there. Only later did it come to him that he had been using them to polish the windscreen.

As it happened, though, the Mercedes was off the road for the moment while the garage did something to its insides, and Sebastian was using a hired car to get about. To Partridge's disgust, he had rented a Ford Capri for the week, an ugly beige thing that stood out like a pearly king at a funeral in the officers' car park. No self-respecting guardsman could entertain his girlfriends in such a machine. Partridge was embarrassed even to go near it.

'After all, it's just not a gentleman's car, is it?' he said reproachfully. 'Not what an officer ought to drive. I wouldn't use it, sir, if I was you. I'd take a taxi.'

Lunch in the mess that day was a cheerful noisy affair, a symphony of clinking glasses and popping champagne corks. The parade had gone without hitch. After drinking his share of Krug, even the Adjutant, still wearing his frock coat, allowed that he had once seen men on crutches do worse. At the other end of the room, the newly-commissioned young ensigns, who preferred to keep their distance from the Adjutant, brightened at this information. On their shoulders would his displeasure have fallen if it had been otherwise.

Sebastian joined the party in time to watch the lunch-time news on television. It was a repeat of the morning's events. Film of the parade was followed by footage of the Royal Family on the balcony of Buckingham Palace, waving to the crowd while RAF jets swept low overhead. The next item was of particular interest. It showed scenes of rioting Catholics in Derry, long-haired youths chanting Republican slogans and hurling milk bottles at a harassed platoon of soldiers, Green Jackets by the look of them, who were trying to keep order. 'If you kill a British soldier, clap your hands,' sang the demonstrators:

'If you kill a British soldier, clap your hands,
If you kill a British soldier, kill a British soldier,
If you kill a British soldier, clap your hands.'

'Some four thousand Roman Catholics rioted in Londonderry earlier today,' explained the newscaster, *'in protest at what they called "unnecessary provocation" by the Protestant community. Stones were thrown at troops, and an RUC station was besieged for several hours. Although several casualties were reported, officials said later that the situation was now under control. An SDLP spokesman deplored the incidents and called on the rioters to return to their homes.*

'Abroad now, and from British Casuarina reports are coming in…'

Sebastian didn't stay to watch any more. He had seen enough. It was a short step from throwing milk bottles to mixing Molotov cocktails; once they began to burn cars and put up barricades, nothing short of a massive display of strength would restore order to the town. Sebastian had been in the army long enough to know that when the authorities announced that the situation was under control, it was time to pack a kitbag and put his shaving tackle where he could get at it in a hurry. Unless he was badly mistaken, it would be the night ferry from Liverpool for 9 Platoon that evening. The men had better be told.

The last will and testament of 243981965 Guardsman Turtle P. was a thin document, a single sheet of paper, written in biro on Form

MOD 106 ('If you cannot write you must make your mark'). There was not much to it. Turtle had no money and no worldly goods. Everything he possessed, the regiment had given him.

It was the division of these military spoils after his demise that had aroused his concern. Like most Guardsmen, either by stealth or guile, Turtle had succeeded in acquiring a collection of soldierly articles over and above his entitlement. He was determined that this collection should not revert to the army on his death.

'I've got some extra kit, see,' he confided to Sebastian. 'A waterproof torch and a commando knife, sir, one of the good ones with a knuckleduster grip. You can't get hold of them nowadays.' He spoke as if he was an old man. 'They're mine. It's not right for the army to have them when I go. I want to leave them to Partridge without him knowing. He's my mate, see, but he'd laugh at me if I told him. Know what I mean?'

Sebastian knew. 'Fair enough. But what about your civilian things? Your personal effects. What d'you want done with those?' Among Turtle's personal effects were a drawerful of comics and two model aeroplanes – one a Stuka, the other a Spitfire – which hung from string above his bed.

'Throw 'em away. They won't be no good to me. Not after I'm gone.' Turtle fastened trusting eyes on his platoon commander. Sebastian felt as if he, personally, had just arranged Turtle's execution. 'But I want Partridge to have the knife and the torch. All legal, like. That's why I asked for you, sir, to look at my will. You're good with words.'

Better, at any rate, than Turtle. His education had been derived in large part from watching television. For as long as he could remember, he had had no father to speak of and a mother who, though she loved him, had proved inadequate to the task of bringing him up. He had spent most of his life in a children's home and indeed was still technically in the care of the local authority. Next week, on his eighteenth birthday, the commanding officer would sign for him and he would become the official responsibility of the army.

Until then he was merely on loan, a gift to the nation as it were, from the Mayor and Corporation of Wolverhampton.

He had been with the battalion only a few weeks. An upholsterer by trade, he had drifted into an army recruiting office in Wolverhampton with vague ideas of driving a tank. These had been dispelled by a fast-talking Gobelin sergeant who admired his height and escorted him on to the London train before he knew what was happening. Several months later, after being back-squadded during basic training at the Guards depot, Turtle, soldier of the Queen, had reported for duty at 9 Platoon.

There was no doubt in his mind as to why he had joined the Guards. No doubt at all. Others enlisted because they were broke, bored or pursued by pregnant women – sometimes all three. Not Turtle. He was in it for the glamour.

'I want to be a soldier, sir,' he had informed Sebastian, the first time they met. 'I really do. It's better than being an upholsterer. Stuffing chairs all day long. It's healthy, too. Fresh air and exercise – and action, sir, plenty of action. That's what it's all about.'

Sebastian spent the rest of the afternoon going through his kit piece by piece, checking every item to make certain it would do the job it was supposed to. He told himself that one hundred per cent efficiency was essential. He took his rifle apart and cleaned the mechanism, then gave it a light coating of oil before wiping it dry. There would be no time for such niceties when he was flat on his belly in the Creggan, wondering which of five hundred windows hid the sniper who had just killed the man standing next to him. He checked everything – boots, bootlaces, buttons, field dressing, water bottle, back pack and straps, all the minutiae of soldiering, all the trivial insignificant things that Partridge should have done. If his equipment let him down, it would be nobody's fault but his own.

When he had finished, he went across to the barrack room to see if the platoon had followed his example. They had. Under Sergeant Ball's direction, their kitbags had been stacked neatly by the door and they were sprawled on their beds, ready to crash out as soon as the telephone rang. Any excuse would do. Even a terrorist scare at London Airport, a hysterical Arab threatening to blow himself up, would be better than nothing.

That was the chief danger, that nothing would happen. The Guardsmen were prepared for combat, even looking forward to it. They were nerved up to face the worst: an Armalite rifle pointing at their back perhaps, or a green wire in a South Armagh hedgerow, or an abandoned car with locked boot or – worst of all – a gang of wall-to-wall Catholic women surrounding a lone soldier in a cul-de-sac. Ireland, they could handle. It was the unknown that worried them. As Turtle explained it, talking of the riots in Derry: 'I'd rather be over there than here. Me personally. It gets on my tits just sitting around this place.'

Nevertheless, it was plain to Sebastian that morale in the platoon was higher than it had been all year. Even the arrival of a civilian with a black briefcase, who earned his living by selling life insurance to soldiers on Spearhead, failed to dampen 9 Platoon's spirits. The prospect of active service – of danger, discomfort and perhaps even death – did more to arouse them than even a home win for Spurs. This was borne out by the appearance on recent mornings of many unfamiliar faces at roll call. During the spring months, an endless round of guard rosters and barrack fatigues had pushed the tally of absentees without leave to absurd heights. Half the battalion had been engaged travelling all over the kingdom to bring back errant comrades under escort. Excuses ranged from 'I missed the last train, sir' (for an absence of three weeks) to 'Well sir, there was this girl…' But Spearhead had changed all that. The level of absentees had flickered briefly and then dropped to zero. Not one member of the Gobelin Guards was now being hunted by police. No one wanted to miss getting his head blown off along with his mates. Guardsmen the battalion never knew it possessed had appeared out of nowhere with a sheepish grin and were now in barracks, sitting on their hands and waiting for something to happen, as happen it surely would.

The day wore on. Soon it was evening. Whenever he had nothing else to do – about every half an hour – Sebastian manufactured an excuse to visit the Orderly Room to see if he could learn anything from the clerks hunched importantly over their typewriters. Twice he watched a Landrover arrive from London District HQ bearing a sealed envelope for the Commanding Officer's eyes only – but whatever the envelopes contained, it was not the order to go. Back in the mess, waiting for dinner, he slid behind a copy of *Horse and Hound* and sat watching the telephone, wishing it would ring. Other officers joined him, flicking restlessly through magazines or else rolling billiard balls back and forth along the green baize table, chalking their cues and waiting impatiently for the call. But none came.

By eight o'clock the BBC had revealed the depressing information that all was now sweetness and light again in Derry. No barricades, no burning cars, no incidents of any sort. Under the circumstances, and in heavy contrast to lunch, dinner was very muted. Nobody felt like talking. Everyone watched the Commanding Officer, searching his face for clues – but though he did his best to look informed, the Commanding Officer knew no more than anyone else. He kept his peace until coffee was served, then removed himself to his armchair in the ante-room to play ludo with the Adjutant. Several officers followed. Others lingered for a while, Sebastian among them, until Lord Malplaquet began to tell stories over the brandy. Malplaquet's stories always ended in the same vein '... and a mortar bomb was seen to fall on the married quarters'. Once he got started, most officers settled for bath and an early bed. Sebastian went too. He had no reason to stay up. It had been a long day, and it was clear that nothing was going to happen tonight. The evening was ending in frustration.

The word came at five next morning. Partridge brought it. He pushed open the door without ceremony and shook Sebastian's head against the pillow until he was awake.

'Get up, Mr Clinch,' he said. 'We're on our way. We've got orders to move.'

Sebastian was out of bed already. 'Where is it? Derry?'

'No sir, not Derry.' Partridge looked worried. 'Somewhere else, somewhere I haven't heard of. Bit of a turn up, actually.' He sniffed. 'It's a shooting job, apparently, in a place called British Casuarina. Wherever that is.'

3

The Commanding Officer's reaction to the news became a military legend. At nine a.m., as soon as the shops were open, he pushed a troubled face around the door of his office and stuffed a five-pound note into the hands of the nearest Orderly Room clerk with instructions to go up to Sloane Square and purchase a map of the world from W. H. Smith's. The clerk was back in ten minutes carrying an atlas. A search of the index thereupon revealed the exact location of British Casuarina.

It was in the Indian Ocean. An island, or rather one third of one, off the coast of Madagascar, marked with an arrow and the words (*To GB and France*) in italic lettering. A broad pink oval in the sea midway between Mauritius and the Seychelles, sharing a border across the island with the much larger nation of Santa Monica. One of the last Anglo-French colonies in the southern hemisphere.

Indeed British Casuarina (or Casuarina Français, as it was known on French maps) would have dropped the colonial ties long ago if it wasn't for the territorial ambitions of the Santa Monican regime. Santa Monica wished to unite the whole island under its flag. At the beginning of the 1960s, Britain and France had made Casuarina an offer of independence. As long as Santa Monica pressed its claim, however, the Casuarina Legislative Council preferred to retain its defence links with the parent countries, for reasons of necessity rather than sentiment.

Every now and again – and this was one of the occasions – Santa Monica's posturing on the land issue flared into a positive threat of invasion. Even as the Commanding Officer pored over his atlas, Santa Monican troops and guns were said to be moving up into the jungle along the disputed border, poised to smash through the hundred-strong Casuarina Defence Force and drive it into the sea. It was no coincidence that the Santa Monican *escudo* had been devalued by fifty per cent that same week. By cutting the pay packet of the armed forces in half, the ruling junta had obliged itself to divert attention from its domestic problems by uniting the people in a national crusade for the honour of the republic. The people of Santa Monica were volatile and trigger-happy – most cinema screens in the country were made of concrete to discourage the audience from participating in shoot-outs. A national crusade, whether for honour or not, would be prosecuted with fervour.

None of this was apparent to Sebastian as he pulled on his clothes that morning. Several days were to pass before the full story filtered down to him. In common with Partridge, he knew nothing about British Casuarina and cared less. All that mattered was that Derry, recently so large on the horizon, had been struck off the itinerary. Alleluia! It seemed too good to be true.

Outside his bedroom window, he could hear a lone musician marching through barracks playing reveille on a fife. Three centuries ago the tune *Stand to, Gobelins,* played at dawn by an alert drummer boy, had saved the sleeping regiment from certain annihilation by Boufflers' army. Ever since, it had been a Gobelin tradition to waken the battalion the same way on the morning of a change of quarters. So the musician was out in the half-darkness, wearing his bearskin, rousing the troops to arms. Thus had the battalion loaded its wounded onto wagons and moved out of Minden, Malplaquet (the place, not the Earl) and Tel-el-Kebir. Thus had it withdrawn from Mons and Dunkirk, hurriedly but with dignity. Thus had it advanced day by day across North Africa from El Alamein to Tunis. Now it was moving again, from a comfortable billet in London to an unknown destination the other side of the Equator.

Sebastian shaved swiftly and headed across the road to the barrack block. Sergeant Ball was already there. He was torn between pleasure at the prospect of leaving Mrs Ball and annoyance at the extra work it entailed.

'It's Turtle's feet,' he declared. 'They're enormous. And different sizes. I can't indent for a pair of jungle boots with less than six months' warning, sir. The army *knows* that.'

The army did indeed. Turtle's feet – one size thirteen, the other twelve – were a long-standing problem.

'Have you tried the Quartermaster?' Sebastian asked.

'Yes, sir. He's doing what he can, but there's not much chance in the time available.'

'Where are the men now?'

'They're down there, sir, drawing a full issue of jungle kit. You too, sir, when you're ready.'

The Quartermaster's stores had been thrown open to the battalion. In one door filed a long queue of soldiers dressed in the combat kit they had been expecting to wear in Northern Ireland; out of the other they emerged festooned with hammocks, mosquito nets, machetes and water-sterilising tablets. Each carried a plastic bag containing three more plastic bags, a small medical kit, a bottle of insect repellent, a sharpening stone, a tin of foot powder and a cloth bag designed to recycle drinking water from urine. Above their heads the skylights had been blotted out by a mountain of tropical equipment reaching up to the ceiling. The mountain represented the fruit of much imaginative paperwork by the Quartermaster and his staff. Little by little it was shrinking to nothing as the troops passed across it in search of booty. The Quartermaster, true to his kind, was inconsolable.

It was the same at the cookhouse, where Sebastian went to see up the men's breakfast before he had his own. From behind his gleaming empire of pots and pans, the Master Cook emerged in a vile humour. Trembling with annoyance he strode between the chip-frying machines, clutching in his fist a note commanding him to transform six hundred hot lunches into six hundred picnic bags for distribution by 0900 hours. The Master Cook wasn't a bloody magician. He swore he would purchase his discharge that very day. He had his pension, he told his underlings. He would open his own restaurant and never take sodding orders from the sodding army ever again. Ever.

In the high-rise married quarters behind the company lines, troops broke the news to their wives like millions before them, some weeping in their hearts and some rejoicing. One or two wives bore it calmly; most took the chance to assault their spouse with frying pan or broom handle or china duck. A few wept on the necks of their men. Others, shrill with triumph, made no secret of their feelings. They couldn't wait to see the back of their husbands. Exactly so had the regiment set out to fight the war of Jenkins' Ear and that of the Peninsula; exactly so had its womenfolk responded.

Grievance and complaint arose on every front, filling the air with unconcealed resentment. Angry wives demanded an interview with the Commanding Officer and were hushed into silence by tremulous husbands. Soldiers whose new jungle greens didn't fit, cursed and swore. Drivers from the MT park emerged reluctantly from underneath their vehicles and were only persuaded to co-operate in this new venture on the promise of another vehicle, just as immaculate, at the other end. The wine waiter wondered gloomily if his cash fiddle would survive the upheaval in the officers' mess. The battalion butcher was certain his wouldn't. Moan moan in the cookhouse, moan moan in the company lines, moan moan in the Orderly Room, moan moan in the Pay Office and the armoury and the signals wing, moans everywhere, loud and clear and querulous. The battalion hadn't been so happy in a long time.

First, Spearhead or no Spearhead, there were a number of rituals to be observed before the Gobelin Guards could set out for foreign parts. One of these was Company Orders.

Company Orders took place every morning in the Company Commander's office. It was a formal parade to discuss the business of the day, most of which was usually taken up with punishing the previous day's wrongdoers. It was presided over by the Earl of Malplaquet.

Sebastian hurried into the office and took his place beside Malplaquet's desk.

'You!' said the Company Commander. There was outrage in his voice.

'Sir?' Because this was technically a parade, Malplaquet and Sebastian called each other 'you' and 'sir'. At other times they were supposed to use Christian names. By mutual consent, they both preferred 'you' and 'sir'.

'That thing in the car park.'

What thing? What was he talking about?

'That dirt-coloured object. That motor car.'

Ah. Malplaquet had spotted the hired Ford.

'I can explain,' began Sebastian. 'My own car...'

'Explain! Explain what? I don't want explanations. I want results. That car does not belong in the officers' car park. You will remove it at once. You will not drive it again. Clear?'

'Clear, sir.' There was no point arguing. Malplaquet's views on gentlemen's transport were not flexible.

He referred to a note on his blotter. 'You have a Guardsman Turtle in your platoon?'

'Yes sir.'

'I've just had a long-distance telephone call from his mother in Wolverhampton, or some such place. I found it hard to understand what she was trying to tell me – she appeared to be coming to the point, when her money ran out – but she sounded excited. I gather she didn't want her son to go abroad. Something about him being too young.'

'Well, he is rather.'

'It's a chance for him to earn his pay.' Malplaquet put on his cap and nodded curtly. 'Let's get on with Orders.'

Sebastian opened the door and passed the word to Sergeant Ball, who was waiting outside with the Company defaulters. There was only one. Yesterday's exertions had left the men little time or energy to get themselves into trouble. Gilligan, alone, stood in the passage, pressed of uniform and expressionless of face.

'Orders!' yelled Ball. 'Company orders, *shun*! Quick march! Derft right, derft right, derft right! Mark time! Halt!'

Gilligan was now standing in front of the desk, eyes focused on the wall above Malplaquet's head. He remained silent and aloof as Sergeant Ball read out the charge against him, which alleged that he had been absent from a swabbing session in the barrack room.

Ball explained it. 'At 1500 hours yesterday, sir, after dinner was over, I ordered all the Guardsmen of number 9 Platoon to swab out the barrack room consequent to us going on Spearhead. At 1515 hours I took a head count and noticed that the accused was missing. I then went into the latrines, where I observed cigarette smoke coming from one of the toilets. I asked who was in there. On receiving no reply, I investigated further and discovered the accused. Sir.'

Malplaquet brooded over the charge sheet. He had the unlettered man's respect for legal jargon. It was some time before he spoke.

'Gilligan.'

'Sir.'

'Is this true?'

'Yes sir.'

Malplaquet turned to Sebastian. 'How has Gilligan been behaving in the platoon?'

Sebastian had his answer ready. 'I have been his platoon commander for eighteen months now, sir, and I have always found him reliable, hard-working and eager to please.'

Gilligan's ears burned at this description of himself. His eyes flickered from side to side, wondering if Sebastian had slipped off his trolley at last. Sebastian's assessment was palpably false, as everyone in the room knew. True, Gilligan had once volunteered for service in Belfast – but only to avoid being cross-posted to public duties in the 2nd battalion. He disliked public duties. The last time he had been on guard at Windsor Castle, he had manhandled an ancient cannon over the battlements in the middle of the night, in the belief that the army would grant him a free discharge. Anyone less eager to please would have been hard to find.

Sebastian had reasons of his own for singing Gilligan's praises. He was prisoner's friend, for one, and Malplaquet's behaviour over the hired car had irritated him. This was his chance to get even.

Malplaquet did not look at Sebastian again. 'All the same, Gilligan, it's not good enough, not good enough at all. This is the second or third time you've come before me this month.' He glanced at Ball for confirmation.

'Fourth, sir,' said Ball.

'Four times too many.' Malplaquet consulted the punishment book, where Ball had already pencilled in a scale of possible punishments against Gilligan's name. 'You will do four extra fatigues,' he announced. It was the maximum allowable for the offence. 'They are to be paid off the *moment* we get to British Casuarina. And I don't want to catch you in here again.' He closed the book with a snap and waved everyone away. 'March out!'

Footsteps echoed in double time down the passage, a door slammed, then there was silence. Lord Malplaquet was alone. Leaning forward, he picked up the papers on his desk and rearranged them in neat uniform piles, according to size. He was thoughtful. He could not conceal a small frown of dissatisfaction at the way the day was shaping up. The business of the car had been one thing; Gilligan another; and now there was this move, and all the trouble it created.

Malplaquet was undecided about British Casuarina. He shared the common enthusiasm for an excursion overseas, but for different, more personal reasons. He was an ambitious man. He wanted very badly to take command of the battalion when the present Commanding Officer retired in nine months' time. Besides himself, there were two other declared candidates for the job, both currently holding down staff appointments abroad, both – according to the grapevine – making a considerable success of their postings. Lord Malplaquet was coming a poor third in the race. Unless he did something spectacular, he knew he would never make up the lost ground in time, would never see himself adding a further star to the major's crown already upon his shoulder. Unless he did something spectacular.

The more he thought about it, the more the idea of British Casuarina was beginning to grow on Malplaquet. The advantages were obvious. While his rivals occupied themselves with administrative duties, he would be on active service, drawing himself to the attention of the promotion board, keeping the name of Malplaquet squarely in the public eye. Under the circumstances, it was an opportunity not to be missed.

A nicely timed campaign would do wonders for his candidature. Malplaquet was convinced of that. If he acquitted himself well during the coming weeks, if he made his reputation in Casuarina, the powers-that-be could hardly fail to be impressed. They would be forced to sit up and take notice. Properly handled, he was certain he could win them over to his point of view. And then the command – the *command*! – would be his for the taking.

Sebastian used the telephone in the officers' mess to ring up the hire firm and arrange for the collection of his car from barracks. All around hurried waiters, bent on packing the mess chattels into as few boxes as they would go. The two regimental Colours, which normally had pride of place on the dining-room wall, had already been taken down and rolled into tight black leather cases. Each was worth £6000 in gold thread alone. They would travel by air to British Casuarina, there to be unfurled with suitable pomp at battalion headquarters. The silver statues from the dining table were coming too – the Fontenoy grenadier and the Waterloo private, household gods of the battalion. Also a lifesize oil painting of a sulky youth in khaki, a junior ensign who had won the regiment's sole Victoria Cross of the Boer War.

Only one officer, the Adjutant, still remained in the dining room. He was consuming a leisurely breakfast in the midst of chaos. A student of Drake, he believed in setting an example of unruffled calm at all times. From the safety of the serving hatch, a posse of impatient orderlies took it in turns to glare at him, willing him to surrender his knife and fork. The Adjutant took no notice of them, but continued to study his newspaper with fixed gaze.

Sebastian hurried to his room. Partridge was waiting. He had laid out a new set of tropical clothes and was busy repacking a kitbag.

'This is good order,' he declared. 'Us going to British thing. I wonder what the women will be like.'

'More your type than mine, I should think.'

'I heard the French are coming too. Spearhead, same as us.' Partridge fastened a buckle. 'They're flying a battalion out from Paris.'

'Really? Who told you that?'

'Mate of mine in the Orderly Room. Says it's a race who gets there first.'

Rapt in contemplation, Partridge handed over a jungle shirt and a pair of lightweight green trousers. Sebastian took off his shoes and put on a pair of rubber-soled jungle boots, Malaya pattern, which had to be laced halfway up the calf and looked satisfactorily professional. He buckled on his webbing and clipped his belt into position. Round his neck he hung three metal identity discs, each bearing the same information: *4926895 Clinch S. J. CofE. O Pos.* If he should be killed, he knew there would be no poetry spoken over him, no soft words for the passing of a brave man. Instead, one dog tag would be tied around his big toe and another placed between his teeth. The third, with two holes in it, was to be screwed to his coffin.

One final touch and he was ready. From his bedside table he took an oval locket of blue and gold enamel, edged with beadwork. It contained a lock of brown hair attached by two stitches of faded red thread to a piece of white parchment. It was a gift from a famous soldier to one of his ancestors. The reverse carried the inscription: '*F. M. The Duke of Wellington's hair, given 1816 to Honoria, Countess Cadogan*'.

Sebastian buttoned the locket into the top pocket of his shirt. His father and grandfather had both carried it into action with the regiment. Now it was his turn. As they had worn it – in advance and retreat, in shell scrape and dugout – so would he. He could hardly wait.

9 Platoon were standing beside the transport that was to take them to the airbase. A column of covered green lorries stretched from the gate to behind the sergeants' mess, engines ticking over while their drivers supervised the loading of the baggage. Each lorry had its own group of soldiers gathered around the tailboard, carrying their weapons and waiting for the order to embus.

The advance party had already gone. It had left at first light and by now would be several hours airborne, *en route* for British Casuarina, where it was to secure the landing ground and prepare for the arrival of the main body. As soon as the advance party's departure had been officially confirmed, beyond the possibility of recall, the Commanding Officer had said as much in a telegram to the Queen. In time-honoured language, the telegram read: *'With humble duty, all ranks of the 1st battalion Gobelin Guards, on proceeding overseas, send your Majesty Loyal Greetings and assurance of their continued devotion.'*

Sergeant Ball had divided the platoon into three ranks, with the contents of their packs spread out in front of them. He was stepping from man to man, making random checks to ensure that nobody was missing any kit. Except Turtle. As Ball had predicted, it had been impossible to find jungle boots his size. So Turtle was dressed in tropical greens and gleaming drill boots, his smartest pair, the ones he had worn yesterday at the birthday parade.

'Right lad,' said Ball. 'Got your water-purifying pills?'

'Yes, Sarnt. Two different kinds. Blue and white.'

'Good boy. Mess tins?'

'Yes, Sarnt.'

'Scoffing spanners?'

'Sarnt?'

'Knife, fork, spoon. Have you got knife, fork and spoon?'

'Yes, Sarnt. Shall I show them to you?'

'I think you'd better.'

Doubling over to the truck, Turtle retrieved his kitbag and spilled the insides on to the ground. First to drop out were a pair of corporal's chevrons, which tumbled to one side and lay brightly upon the groundsheet for everyone to see. Turtle moved to cover them with his foot, but Sergeant Ball was too quick for him. Ball stared at the stripes with exaggerated interest, then glanced at Turtle.

'What d'you want with those tapes?'

'Dunno, Sarnt.' Turtle had gone the colour of Hampton Court. 'Might come in useful. You never know when you may get made up.'

'Oh yes? You think you're going to be promoted, do you?'

'Fat chance,' put in Partridge.

'Shut it, Partridge! Nobody asked you.' Ball turned back to Turtle. 'All right, lad. Put 'em away. Can't do any harm.' He peered delicately inside the bag. 'What else have you got in there? ... Hallo, a rifle cleaning kit. You did bring a rifle, did you?'

Turtle was offended. 'Of *course*, Sarnt.'

Ball caught Sebastian's eye and grinned. 'Go on,' he told Turtle. 'Hop on the wagon before you get lost.'

Sebastian was glad of Ball. His soldiering went back a long way. He had been in the Guards Parachute Company and had fought the Indonesians in Borneo during the 1960s. He had watched head hunters at work, despatching their Communist enemies and carrying the spoils of war in triumph back to their long-houses. Ball rarely mentioned the Borneo campaign. He had to have several drinks in the sergeants' mess before he would talk about it, and then only if he was in the mood.

From behind the line of trucks appeared the mammoth figure of Lord Malplaquet. Like everyone else, he was dressed in jungle clothing and looked out of place against an urban backdrop of Chelsea flats. His boots were lashed to his calves with a tight bow just below the knee.

'Sarnt Ball,' he said. He did not speak to Sebastian. 'I've just been round the barrack room. I found this.' He produced a screwed-up potato crisp packet.

'Sorry, sir. Must have missed it.'

'Evidently. Have you done a kit check?'

'Yes, sir. It's been done. It's all in hand.'

Malplaquet picked out a tall soldier with a pink face. 'You,' he said. 'Lay out your kit where I can see it.'

For the second time, fulminating under his breath, Turtle unfastened his kitbag and arranged the contents in a neat pile on the ground. He was careful to conceal the corporal's stripes. Bending down, Malplaquet probed for a while but could find nothing amiss. He pronounced himself satisfied. 'Always good to double check,' he said.

A crescendo of pulsating machinery announced the time for departure. Shouldering their back packs, the remaining stragglers clambered aboard. Drivers pushed up tailgates and locked them into place. Peering out, the troops waved to the stony-faced group of wives lining the tarmac and blew kisses to the babies nestling damply in their arms. Rude words, born of envy and regret, were heaped upon the soldiers in the trucks by the unfortunate few detailed to stay behind in the rear party.

It had fallen to Sebastian to be the officer travelling in the first lorry of the column. Striding self-consciously down the line, he made a count of the vehicles and climbed into the passenger seat of the leading three-tonner. On his knee was a map of southern England, the route to the RAF station heavily underlined in red chinagraph. He put his head out of the window. The driver of the following truck was watching over the top of the steering wheel. Waving his arm forward, Sebastian gave the signal to advance.

One by one the lorries picked up speed across the parade ground and lumbered out of the gate into the traffic leading towards Sloane Square. Women in high heels and exotic garb, boutique bound, click-clacked along the kerb as the convoy turned into the King's Road. Heavy diesel fumes almost concealed the news placard outside the underground station. 'BRITISH CASUARINA CRISIS – CRACK TROOPS FLY OUT', it said.

So, in the footsteps of many, the Gobelin Guards went to war.

4

After Mombasa, the Kenya mainland gave way abruptly to the dapple blue waters of the ocean, pale and translucent along the shore, deeper and more placid in the fuller depths outside the reef. At thirty thousand feet the thin white breakers were still clearly visible, hurling themselves endlessly in line abreast against the coral. Puppylike, the aeroplane's shadow passed over them, chasing light-heartedly over sand and reef and diamond-studded water in turn.

Skirting around Cape Amber, the big-bellied transport plane turned south parallel to the coast of Madagascar, then banked to port and began a gradual descent eastwards, deeper and deeper into the Indian Ocean. Somewhere down there steamed the French missile cruiser *Oran*, her warheads armed and ready for firing. Turtle, whose first air trip this was, moved unceasingly from window to window in search of the vessel, but so far had reported no sign of her.

The journey from England had lasted twenty-four hours, broken only by a stop for refuelling in Cyprus and another in Nairobi. 9 Platoon had eaten supper over the Mediterranean and breakfast over the Sudan. In another half hour, give or take a few minutes, they were due to reach their final destination and touch down in British Casuarina.

So far as anyone knew, war had not as yet broken out between Great Britain and the Republic of Santa Monica. The latest intelligence report, delivered by a Foreign Office diplomat who met the plane at Nairobi Airport, stated that although Santa Monican troops were still positioned in strength along the border, no attempt had been made to encroach upon Anglo-French territory. Whether the Santa Monicans were waiting until all their troops had been assembled, or whether they intended to assess the Europeans' reaction before deciding their next move, was anybody's guess.

The Foreign Office official had also given a thumb-nail sketch of Santa Monica, based on the background report his station had telexed to London that morning. The country's history was brief and turbulent. Once Portuguese, it was now independent. Its people – a mixture of Portuguese, Indian and negro – were seventy per cent illiterate. Since the rural areas were obviously ripe for Communist infiltration, either Russian or Cuban, the United States of America maintained a heavy presence across the land, mostly in the form of financial aid and military equipment. A regular supply of outdated military hardware flowed from the US to Santa Monica, enabling the ruling junta to suppress periodic left-wing assaults on its regime. This hardware was now pointing at British Casuarina.

The reasons for Anglo-French involvement in Casuarina remained obscure. The joint administration had always been an uneasy one. It dated from the nineteenth century, based originally upon a shared distrust of the Portuguese, who had never made any secret of their desire to annex the territory and the valuable deep-water port on its southern shore. Although the Portuguese had gone, the deep-water port remained. The new regime in Santa Monica, while rejecting the heritage of colonialism, had freely assumed the territorial aspirations of its former overlords.

The man from the Foreign Office didn't go very deeply into the question of the disputed frontier. Apart from insisting that Britain and France were in the right – legally, anyway – he contented himself with recounting an incident from the past to illustrate the character of the foe. The incident took place in 1979, an election year in Santa Monica. Attended by a coachload of newspaper photographers, a member of the military junta crossed the border into Casuarina and publicly burned a tricolour and a photo of the British Royal Family. He then informed his audience of native Creoles, none of whom spoke Portuguese, that the hour of liberation was at hand. The Creoles hauled him before the town magistrate on a charge of defacing government property. He was bound over to keep the peace, and later escorted back across the border.

'Their bark is worse than their bite,' said Foxtrot, the battalion intelligence officer, who had made his way aft to give the officers an informal briefing before touchdown. 'The Santa Monicans go in for the dramatic gesture, like all Latins, but they rarely follow it up with positive action. They're mostly piss and wind.'

'So what happens next?' asked Lord Malplaquet.

'I wouldn't like to say. They probably don't know themselves.'

'What about the United Nations then?' asked Sebastian. 'Can't they do something?'

'The Santa Monicans have already sent a delegate to the UN reiterating their claim to Casuarina, but it looks as if that was just a cover for their invasion plans. Until they actually cross the border, though, they're doing nothing against international law. All we can do is sit tight and wait for something to happen.'

Foxtrot wasn't the intelligence officer's real name. It was the appointment title by which all such officers could be identified in radio communication. His real name was Captain Duff-Barrington-Gore. This was such a mouthful that he had been known to everyone as Foxtrot since the day he took over the job.

Spearhead had come at an awkward moment for him. Although he dared not tell anyone, he was secretly studying for History A Level in order to resign his commission and read for the Bar. The exam was now but a few weeks away. He had better things to do than become involved in a war.

'I've got a rundown here on the Santa Monican orbat,' he went on. 'I'd like you all to look at it. It's pretty basic. The army consists mainly of infantry, with two squadrons of tanks. Virtually all the soldiers are conscripts. If the invasion does come off, depending on how many troops the French put up, it looks as if they could outnumber us by about four to one.'

He turned a page in his file. 'There's the air force to consider, too. Most of it is junk by modern standards. But the fact remains, until the *Oran* gets within effective range, that we have no anti-aircraft weapons of our own. No Rapiers, no ack ack guns, nothing. They've caught us on the hop.'

Foxtrot closed the file and handed it to the Adjutant. The Commanding Officer had already seen it. In strict order of seniority it passed from hand to hand until it arrived, towards the end, on Sebastian's lap. The file contained photographs of Santa Monican weapons and artillery, an estimate of their capabilities, and a list of heavy armaments known to have been supplied to them by the United States military-industrial complex. The section on the air force was especially informative.

FORCA AEREA DE SANTA MONICA

Helicopters	3 Sikorsky H-19
Transport aircraft	6 Douglas C-47
	1 Douglas C-54
Ground attack aircraft	8 Cessna A-37B (converted for strafing)
	8 North American (Cavalier) F-51D
	12 Mustang P51B

'These Mustangs,' said Sebastian. 'Aren't they the fighter planes the Americans used during the war?'

'They are indeed,' Foxtrot replied. 'As soon as they became obsolete, the Yanks sold them off cheap to whoever would buy them, or even gave them away free. Most of them are still in service under their new owners.'

Sebastian read on: '*Santa Monica has no navy. The army consists of 5000 men equipped with automatic weapons and self-loading rifles. Several battalions are mechanised with half-track vehicles, supported by two fully operational squadrons of Sherman tanks.*'

Shermans, yet! Second War Shermans! Sebastian glowed. This was going to be better than he had expected.

'I don't know what they mean by "fully operational",' Foxtrot concluded. 'Those tanks are an unknown quantity. The men who drive them are supposed to have been trained in the States, but they appear to have had very little practical experience. Almost none, in fact. Santa Monica is mostly hills and jungle, so there's not much room for an armoured squadron to deploy. As far as I can gather, the tanks are a prestige weapon as much as anything. They're for show. They've only been into action once – and that was to put down a riot in the capital. It's impossible to say what they'd be like in a real war.'

Casuarina International Airport – international because it ran a connecting service to Nairobi – was shimmering in the noonday heat. Almost before the aircraft had been directed on to blocks, an elderly negro baggage loader shuffled forward and sat down to rest in the shadow of the wing. A blast of putrid, swamp-fed air met 9 Platoon through the opened hatch. Stumbling into bright sunlight, which contrasted strongly with the gloom of the aircraft's whalelike interior, they formed up on the asphalt in front of a large sign proclaiming for the benefit of tourists 'Bienvenue à Casuarina'. In happier times the airport would have been thronged with visitors from Europe and South Africa. Within the last twenty-four hours, however, all non-essential civilian flights had been cancelled until further notice.

A brief ceremony took place as the two junior ensigns of the battalion marched down the aircraft ramp bearing the regimental Colours at an angle on their shoulders. There was no breeze to disturb the limp material of the twin standards. Smartly the escort of Guardsmen presented arms, then turned outwards with rifles at the high port. The arrival of the Gobelin Guards abroad was now official.

9 Platoon looked around. In front of them, a weather-beaten control tower loomed over a long low building of dirty brown stone, once white, which was the international departure lounge. Coils of new barbed wire had been scattered around it in random, patternless heaps. Beyond the wire, the main airport runway extended some half a mile into the sea, supported on blocks of coral and flanked each side by a column of landing lights mounted on stilts in the water.

A party of sunburned French *poilus*, members of the permanent garrison, were stripped to the waist, hard at work on the runway. They were filling sandbags, digging mortar pits and building sangars. The runway was evidently to be defended against both air and ground attack. Its most obvious landmark was the lighthouse on a mole at the seaward end, a tall red and white structure easily identifiable from a distance. Six men under a *sous-officier* could be seen repainting the tower in irregular shades of blue and green to break up its distinctive shape. Along the sea-shore, a makeshift network of shelter bays and battle trenches was being improvised to allow for both enfilading and defilading fields of fire. The most important of them had already been fitted with overhead cover of solid coral, concealed beneath a tangled mesh of loose camouflage netting.

The international departure lounge, which also served as an arrival hall, was deserted and smelled strongly of decay. It was dominated by a large painted poster of a Gobelin Guardsman on sentry duty outside Buckingham Palace. 'Come to London' exhorted this caricature, beaming toothily at the empty room. Its style was straight Moss Bros.

'Sod that for a laugh,' said Sergeant Ball.

At the door, a restless grey-haired man was waiting to meet the officers. He wore the uniform of an RAF Group Captain and introduced himself as the Garrison Commander of British Casuarina. He had driven down earlier in the day from garrison headquarters at Fort Pitt. With barely a word he led the way at once to an open-sided tent about fifty yards away, specially erected on a patch of exposed ground where no one could eavesdrop. A fresh notice declared it to be the briefing tent. At one end a map of the island had been hung on a blackboard, next to a box of coloured drawing-pins. Facing it were several rows of canvas chairs with their backs to the sun.

Until the events of the past few days, the Garrison Commander had long been looking forward to the end of a two-year tour of duty in British Casuarina, where he had been put out to grass as the last posting of an unspectacular career. His service life had begun uneventfully, continued ditto, and until now had been petering out in the methodical pursuit of butterflies, of which the island had a great many. Commanding the Fort Pitt garrison, which was shared in rotation between English and French, had not hitherto been regarded as a difficult assignment. The garrison normally consisted of a few dozen assorted European troops and a part-time volunteer unit of a hundred ragged natives, the Casuarina Defence Force, most of whom had enlisted for free meals. The European soldiers were specialists – engineers, carpenters, signallers – and could scarcely muster an infantryman between them. The natives had largely gone missing at the first hint of trouble.

For years the Garrison Commander had been savouring the prospect of his retirement pension and an undemanding job as secretary of a golf club in Surrey. Now, to his consternation, he found himself in a situation that was most definitely not to his liking. The idea of being responsible for the defence of British Casuarina left him numb with apprehension. Not of physical danger – for he was no coward – but of making a balls-up of a task which he judged to be beyond his capabilities.

He wasted little time in a speech of welcome. The sooner the Gobelin Guards were in their positions of defence, the more relaxed he would feel. Tapping his cane on the blackboard for silence, he launched into his battle plan without further ceremony. It was the third briefing the officers had heard that day.

'As I see it, the situation is this,' he began. 'The Santa Monicans can attack in one of two ways. They can mount a full-scale frontal assault with tanks and infantry across the border. Or they can make a parachute drop onto certain key installations inside the country, chief of which would be this airfield. We'll take the border first.

'There is only one road between Santa Monica and Casuarina. It crosses a river at the frontier town of Mango Creek, a hundred miles along the coast from here. The jungle beside the road is of considerable strategic importance.' The Garrison Commander took a blue drawing-pin from his box and stuck it into Mango Creek. 'A single platoon will be sufficient to defend the bridge at Mango Creek. I sent a detachment of Royal Engineers up there last night to lay demolition charges so that the bridge can be destroyed at short notice if necessary, thus bringing the Santa Monican armour to a standstill. It ought to be a straightforward operation.

'The other problem is the airfield. The Santa Monicans are known to have a limited number of trained paratroops in their army – about three hundred – so it's conceivable that they might attempt to capture this landing ground and hold it long enough for the rest of their troops to fly in by transport plane. And once on the ground, they could create all sorts of nasties for us this far inside the country.'

The Garrison Commander wiped his face. 'What I intend to do is this. So as not to provide the enemy with any unnecessary provocation – no excuses to invade – I shall send only one company into a forward location in the Mango Creek area. That will be...?' He looked towards the Gobelin Commanding Officer.

'That'll be Blenheim Company under Lord Malplaquet,' said the Commanding Officer, stirring in his seat.

'... Battle Group Blenheim. The rest of the battalion will remain here, in reserve, to defend the airport. The airport is the key to this sort of operation. Our own paras proved that at Suez in 1956. As long as we retain control of the runway, we shall be in a position to dictate events, rather than the other way about.'

Using the remainder of his blue drawing-pins, the Garrison Commander circled the runway on the map with a neat cluster of friendly forces. Then he turned back to face his audience.

'There are the French to consider, too. They're sending an infantry battalion, as you probably know, but they've run into overflying problems and won't be here for a few hours yet. Paris has asked us to hold back and do nothing until their troops do arrive. So it's important that we push ahead with all speed, try and get this thing sewn up before their feet touch the ground.'

A murmur of assent swept through the audience. The officers were impatient to begin. Turning round once more, the Garrison Commander took up a handful of red pins and distributed them at random in the jungle around Mango Creek.

'One final point, gentlemen, before you disperse. The border with Santa Monica, as I'm sure you realise, is really nothing more than a line drawn on a map a hundred years ago. In practical terms, there is no division at all. As far as the people who live there are concerned, the jungle one side is very much the same as the jungle the other side. There's a maze of hidden footpaths leading from villages in Casuarina to villages in Santa Monica and back again, used mostly by Tamil Indians or maroons who know nothing about international politics and wouldn't care if they did. All they want is to be left alone to get on with the main preoccupation of their lives – smuggling ganja.

'Ganja is the local name for marijuana. It is grown by native farmers in Santa Monica and smuggled across the border and down to the sea, where it is shipped out on cargo vessels to Florida and New England. The smuggling operation is tightly controlled by a small army of negro and mulatto gangsters, probable strength fifty to seventy-five, who effectively dominate the jungle on both sides of the frontier. They carry weapons and have been known to use them – in fact we've reason to believe that the Santa Monican government is keeping them supplied with small arms to provide an additional thorn in our flesh. These gangsters are involved in the local cult of Gris Gris, a sort of religion, and are known as Warlocks because of their long spiky hair. They are led by a young black in his late twenties or early thirties, a rabble rouser whose real name is probably Leon Sullivan, though he goes under several different aliases.'

There were no more pins in the box. Stepping back, the Garrison Commander surveyed his handiwork.

'That about wraps it up. As long as they keep out of our way, the Warlocks are not our problem. Quite frankly, it's for the local police to keep an eye on marijuana smuggling. It's nothing to do with the armed forces. Our job is simply to contain the Santa Monican invasion, if it ever comes.'

Dark patches of moisture had begun to glisten across his shoulders and underneath the arms of his light fawn uniform. Behind him the distant hum of twin aircraft engines, which had been gently nagging for some time, came closer on the swamp air. Presently a six-seater Beechcraft Baron appeared over the palm trees and nosed down uncertainly onto the runway. The officers craned their necks to watch it.

'That'll be the BBC from Nairobi,' said the Garrison Commander. 'London told me they were coming.' He looked round. 'I take it there are no questions at this stage? Good. If you'll excuse me then, I'll go and liaise with the media.'

He ducked out of the tent and stepped on to the runway, where the television men were assembling their equipment. Director, front man, cameraman and sound recordist were scrutinising the defence preparations with a professional eye. At the rear, a short vigilant man in zip-up boots and a safari hat emerged from the aircraft and stretched himself before joining the others. He wore tinted spectacles and long hair which coiled snakelike onto his collar. His suit, of a pale tropical material, had been mass-produced – and for someone thinner. It was obvious, just by looking at him, that he came from the suburbs of some large city.

The Garrison Commander greeted the new arrivals warmly. It was important to maintain good relations with the press. He shook hands with everyone, then took a map from his pocket. The men from the BBC gathered round. Jabbing at the map with his forefinger, he began to explain the situation to them in low urgent tones.

After a while, the man in the safari hat buried a yawn, picked up his bag and wandered over towards the briefing tent. For a few seconds he gazed in frank disbelief at the odd little tableau of Guardsmen gathered protectively around the Colours. Then he turned to the officers.

'Hogan is my name,' he announced, addressing himself to no one in particular. 'Willie Hogan, foreign correspondent for the *Daily Tale*. I hitched a lift with the Beeb from Nairobi. Where's the war, gentlemen?'

Foxtrot, who was nearest, assumed spokesmanship for the group. 'You're from the press?'

'I certainly am. The first to arrive, by the look of things. I presume there's no one here yet from the *Guardian* or the *Telegraph*?'

'Not that we know of.'

'Excellent!' Hogan rotated a full circle before taking out his notebook. 'I see you're preparing airport defences. Are you expecting air raids? A parachute drop? I understand the pilots of the Santa Monican air force have sworn on the statue of the founder of the republic to die for their country rather than suffer defeat.'

He knew more than his listeners.

'What about the *Oran*?' he continued. 'Will her Exocets be used against the Santa Monicans? Are the French planning a pre-emptive strike? Where are your anti-aircraft guns? How many…'

'I really think you ought to talk to the Garrison Commander rather than anyone else,' said Foxtrot. 'Things go so much better if they're done through the proper channels, don't you agree?'

'Is it true the airport radar system isn't manned after dark?' Hogan persisted. 'I can't believe it. What happens if the Santa Monicans decide to put on a night landing?'

Foxtrot made the mistake of being drawn. 'It's hardly likely that the Santa Monicans would have an effective night-flying capability.'

'They might! The Israelis did at Entebbe. There's nothing to stop them having a go. What exactly will you do if a fleet of hostile aircraft drops on you in the middle of the night?'

'This isn't Entebbe. And we aren't Ugandans.' Foxtrot was emphatic. 'The situation here is entirely different.'

'I take it you removed that thing from the car park,' said Malplaquet. It was the first time he had spoken to Sebastian since leaving London.

'The car hire people came and took it away. I saw them myself.'

'Good.' Malplaquet's ginger curls and death-white skin were already suffering agonies under the tropical sun. Globules of sweat trembled on his moustache as he talked. 'Now – about the Company's move to Mango Creek. Number 9 Platoon – that's yours – is to be the point platoon for the time being, with numbers 7 and 8 in reserve, alongside Company HQ. We'll dig in behind you, straddling the route to the airport. Your mission is to liaise with the Royal Engineers' rep on the Mango Creek bridge and take command of the demolition arrangements. You will then construct a defensive position around the bridge, bearing in mind that you are not to blow it up except as a last resort – only if you have no other means of holding it, in fact.'

Sebastian was pleased. There wasn't a platoon commander in the battalion who wouldn't have sold his grandmother into slavery to be up at the front, where the action was. The prospect of being strafed by a Mustang, or of doing an Errol Flynn job on a Sherman tank, had captured the popular imagination. The other officers were openly envious. This was his hour.

'I'll need a map,' he said. 'I don't know how to find Mango Creek.'

'Easy,' answered Malplaquet. 'There's only one road. All you do, apparently, is turn right at the end of the runway and follow the railway line for a hundred miles. You can't miss it.'

5

The entry of the Guards into Mango Creek, 9 Platoon's small footnote in history, was effected a few hours later. Though they came as liberators, they were received not with carillons and church bells, but with a lack of enthusiasm bordering almost on the indifferent.

Sebastian arranged for the vehicles to be left under guard outside town, at the point where the railway line ran out of track, and led the way forward on foot towards the gendarme station in the main square. His first duty was to make a courtesy call on the chief of the Special Branch, who was nominally responsible for the maintenance of law and order in the area. The route lay along Regent Street, both sides of which were lined with a row of mud and wattle *campements* thatched with latanier palm. The houses were of flimsy construction so as to be easily re-erected in the event of a cyclone. Next to each, out of reach of the livestock, stood a miniature grain store on stilts, surrounded in most cases by a litter of discarded coconut husks and the remnants of dried fish. In front of the houses, open sewers formed pools in the road and led downhill towards the river, which served variously as drinking fountain, cesspit and communal bathroom.

Although far from triumphant, 9 Platoon's arrival in the town did not go unnoticed. Small boys marched alongside the Guardsmen and old ladies came to watch from their doorways. Men on the sidewalks and young women in bright headscarves stared in ill-concealed bewilderment. There were no whites in the town. Most of the inhabitants were mulatto or Creole, but one or two were Indian and a handful Chinese. Policy dictated that the hearts and minds of the community should be won over by the army. So, whenever any of the natives smiled, 9 Platoon cracked their own faces in return, repaying the greeting with a synthetic display of warmth that would not have disgraced a travelling circus.

Whatever illusions Sebastian may have harboured of himself as a latter-day Lord Byron – aristocrat, defender of the weak, protector of the innocent – did not long survive this introduction to Mango Creek. The atmosphere of the place was not romantic. Nor was there any sense of impending disaster, such as he had been led to expect. If anything, the reverse was true, for the prevailing attitude appeared to be one of calm and quiescence. The main square was crowded with people going about their business in apparent ignorance of the dramatic events which had brought 9 Platoon to their side. The square contained the town's only stone building, which served the dual functions of Customs-house and gendarmerie. A Union Jack and a Tricolour flew in tandem from the tin roof. The only other item of interest that Sebastian could see was a red pillar box with the Queen's initials on it, dwarfed by the feathery green leaves of a filao tree. Nearby a notice warned: 'Dump no night soil here.'

This then was the town that 9 Platoon had come to save, the tiny settlement five thousand miles from London that was to be defended against all comers. A few hundred yards further on, Great Britain's imperial mandate came to a stop against a neglected signpost indicating the frontier with Santa Monica. To Sebastian, still nursing a sense of destiny, the signpost was full of significance. Its function was immemorial. Much as Roman officers, peering into Scotland over the top of Hadrian's Wall, had marked it 'Caledonia – land of barbarians' on their maps, so now he and his troops had carried the imperial leash to full stretch. In a far-flung empire, 9 Platoon was farthest flung of all.

The bridge across the river, too, was a familiar sight. Sebastian recognised it at once from a dozen war movies. Arnhem, Kwai, Remagen – the cinema industry had been this way before. The massive supports were in position, sunk deep into the river bed; and the criss-cross girders, high above the water, carrying the army's lifeline from one bank to the other. It was all there. Nothing had been left out.

The bridge commander turned out to be an absurd youth in jungle shorts and blue stockings, wearing the badges of a Royal Engineers lieutenant. From the pink bloom on his cheeks, he was even younger than Sebastian.

'Pleased to meet you,' he said, extending a damp hand. 'I was wondering when you'd get here. I'm Malcolm Pollock. You weren't at Sandhurst, were you?'

'No, Mons.'

'That's what I suspected. I didn't think I recognised you from the old place.'

So Pollock was a Sandhurst man. From the way he combed his hair forward, Sebastian could see that they would not get on. He was the sort of person who wore sandals in private life. Moreover he was carrying an electrical magazine which he had obviously been reading for pleasure.

'You're going to like the demolition plan we've arranged for you,' he said. 'We've got it all worked out. We'll use slabs of CE-TNT in five different charges with a 1-oz primer and a No 27 detonator. The detonating cord goes off at between 6500 and 8700 yards per second, that's about 15,000 mph. You'll love it!'

His spectacles gleamed in the sunlight.

'What effect will it have on the bridge?'

'It'll twist the girders and distort them beyond all recognition. They'll be so screwed up that the Santa Monicans won't even be able to lift them out and put in new ones. It would be months before they got the bridge working again.'

'And the firing point?'

'Over here.' Pollock led the way to a sand-bagged foxhole beside the road on the Mango Creek side of the river. 'This is where it all happens. As soon as you decide that you can't hold the bridge any longer, you turn the handle and woomph, up she goes. Lovely!'

This was pure Hollywood. Yet Sebastian was conscious of a giant leap back in history. There was nothing new about the bridge at Mango Creek. Horatius, Spurius Lartius and Herminius had

49

encountered much the same problem when defending ancient Rome against Lars Porsena and the Etruscans. As Horatius had been quick to appreciate, the task was essentially one of denying ground of tactical importance to the enemy.

Hew down the bridge, Sir Consul,
With all the speed ye may;
I, with two more to help me,
Will hold the foe in play.
In yon strait path a thousand
May well be stopped by three.
Now who will stand on either hand,
And keep the bridge with me?

'We'll leave the demolitions at State One to begin with,' continued Pollock. 'State One means that they're still safe – the charges are in position, and are wired up and everything, but the detonators have not been connected to the explosive. Once the detonators are put in, then we're at State Two, armed and ready to go.'

Pollock was a disappointment to Sebastian. A definite disappointment. Whatever his specialist skills, and they appeared to be considerable, such a man was hardly the stuff of history. He should not have been at the bridge. His place was elsewhere.

'I'll leave a Sapper NCO behind to command the firing party,' Pollock went on. 'He knows the form. He'll have strict instructions not to blow the bridge until he gets a written order from the commander of the demo guard – that'll be one of your sergeants, presumably. The order should be written on a W4012B and signed in legible handwriting.' Pollock handed over a blank brown form. 'The commander of the demo guard, of course, will take his orders from you, but he won't be authorised to give the go-ahead unless he is in receipt of written instructions with your signature on W4012C.' Pollock produced a yellow form.

Sebastian took it reluctantly. 'All right,' he conceded. 'You'd better show me where the TNT has been positioned, and the firing mechanism, so that I know what the layout looks like.'

'Oh, the demolition charges aren't in position yet. The explosive hasn't arrived. I've indented for it, but I doubt if it'll get here before next week at the earliest.'

'What *has* arrived, then?'

'None of it. No primers, no detonating cord, no safety fuses, nothing. I expect it will all be delivered in the same consignment.'

His message took time to assimilate.

'You mean there's no way right now of destroying the bridge if the Santa Monican armour reaches it?'

'Afraid not. But they know all about it at Fort Pitt. I had a word with them on the radio, and they promised they'd get the equipment up here as soon as it arrives from England. Top priority.'

This was terrible. Looking again at the vast steel and concrete structure spanning the river, Sebastian saw it now with new eyes. What had been entertaining was no longer a joke. He had thirty men to defend it and no help forthcoming. The thought made his stomach curdle.

'What do we do in the meantime?' he asked.

'Well, I'm not an infantryman, mind,' advised Pollock, 'but if I were you I'd commandeer one of those choggy lorries you see driving about and wedge it broadside across the bridge so that no other vehicle can get past. That's the best I can think of. 'Course you'd need the relevant documentation for the owner to claim compensation from the army. I forget what number the form is, but they'd certainly know at Fort Pitt.'

Their van will be upon us
Before the bridge goes down;
And if they once may win the bridge,
What hope to save the town?

'I think that's all I've got to tell you,' Pollock concluded. 'My sappers will handle the electrics and fix all the charges when the equipment does get here. You haven't a thing to worry about on the technical side.' He slipped into the driving seat of his Landrover and closed the door. 'So if you don't need me any more, I'll just head off now. I've a lot to do at Fort Pitt. Buzz me on the radio if there's anything you want to know.' With that, Pollock gave a cheerful wave and was gone.

Sebastian watched the vehicle disappear up the hill. He was alone. Up shit creek, literally, and without a paddle. He felt betrayed. How could the army do this to him?

He gazed at the peaceful river flowing by, at the silent bridge towering above it, at the dense anonymous bushes on the opposite bank from which – at any moment – a horde of swarthy guerrillas flashing cold steel might emerge screaming 'To us the barricades!' Between him and those bayonets there was nothing. Behind him, solid and comforting, were Sergeant Ball and 9 Platoon. Behind them, Lord Malplaquet, Battle Group Blenheim and the rest of the battalion. One way or another, Sebastian had a thousand years of history behind him. He would have preferred something in front.

While waiting for the explosive to arrive, he made a recce of the river bank and set up a defensive position in depth on the reverse and forward slopes, about two hundred yards across the water from the enemy's approaches to the bridge. He sited his three machine guns to provide overlapping arcs of fire on the opposite bank at the point where the advancing infantry would be forced to break cover. To prevent a flanking movement, he placed only two sections forward in slit trenches. The third, less the gun group, he concealed in the rear.

In the middle of the position, on a sharp knoll overlooking the town, lay the ruins of an old sugar planter's house, which had fallen into disuse after the liberation of slaves in the nineteenth century. Sebastian established an observation post at one of the stone windows, facing north towards Santa Monica, from where 9 Platoon had a clear view of a long stretch of road leading to the border, and of the open sea ten miles away down river. Platoon headquarters took shape inside the shell of the building, where Partridge had found a comfortable place to sling his hammock and another – almost as comfortable – to sling Sebastian's. They were joined there by the platoon radio operator, who toiled up the slope with his equipment on his back and erected a ten-foot aerial at the highest point. Switching to a prearranged frequency, he soon established radio contact with Lord Malplaquet at Company HQ and, by relay, with the duty operator at Fort Pitt.

Laying out his compass on the window ledge, Sebastian aligned his map with magnetic north and set out to orientate it against the features he could see on the ground. This was more difficult than he had expected, for the map proved on closer inspection to be an imaginative blend of fact and fiction. A shortage of funds had caused whole areas of the jungle to be left blank. Across them some far away cartographer had stencilled 'No information available'. And worse was to follow. The more he studied the map, the more Sebastian could see that something was wrong with it, badly wrong. It didn't make sense. After puzzling over it some time, he discovered why. A section ten kilometres by ten, with Mango Creek in the middle, had been printed twice and the border drawn in – as far as he could tell – freehand. No wonder the Santa Monicans were upset.

'Here be dragons,' wrote Sebastian. Putting the map away, he drew one of his own, based on what he could see through his field glasses. He took compass bearings of the most prominent features and made an estimate of their range in hundreds of metres. He considered testing these estimates by loosing off a few observed rounds of tracer, but decided against it, reasoning that gunfire this close to the border would not be received by the enemy in the spirit in which it had been intended.

Once the men had dug and camouflaged their own fire trenches, he sent them out with spades and pickaxes to construct anti-tank traps on the Mango Creek side of the bridge, so that if by some mischance the Shermans did succeed in getting across, they would not be able to fan out on either side of the narrow road leading to the sea. It was possible, though unlikely, that 9 Platoon's single Carl-Gustav anti-tank gun would be able to hold the enemy armour in the bottleneck of houses along Regent Street. The first of these traps was the most impressive. It was a wide unbridgeable hole excavated just off the roadside in what had hitherto been somebody's back garden. What the owner thought of it was anybody's guess. A row of female heads had observed the operation from the security of the house's rear windows, but nobody had been out to complain, and Sebastian had no wish to go in and explain himself. He suspected that they would not understand if he said he was digging a hole to catch tanks. It sounded too far-fetched.

As soon as 7 and 8 Platoons were entrenched, Lord Malplaquet drove up to Mango Creek to examine Sebastian's plan of defence. He came, not from down the road, as he should have done, but from behind enemy lines.

At first Sebastian thought the military vehicle approaching from Santa Monica was the spearhead of an invasion force. Through binoculars, however, he saw that it was a signals Landrover with two aerials protruding from either side of the bonnet. It was flying some sort of pennant from the masthead. Covered by a dozen rifles and the anti-tank gun, it crossed the bridge and drew up at the firing point. The pennant resolved itself into a threadbare and much travelled piece of silk, the ancient battle standard of the Malplaquets.

'The map's all to cock,' complained the current warlord. 'I've had hell's own trouble getting here. I asked some soldiers which road to take – home guard, by the look of them – but they were no help. I had to find my own way.'

Sebastian gestured over Malplaquet's shoulder. 'How long were you on that road?'

'About five miles. Why?'

'You must have been in Santa Monica. Those must have been Santa Monican troops.'

'Is that right? It would explain why they didn't salute. Yes, now I come to think of it, there were quite a few of them about. Little brown jobs.'

Sebastian led Malplaquet up the hill and showed him over the position. In general Malplaquet was satisfied with his inspection. But the bridge bothered him.

Sebastian had already attempted to explain the demolition problem to him by radio, using veiled and discreet language that would leave Santa Monican eavesdroppers none the wiser as to the absence of explosive on the bridge. Unfortunately his language had been so cryptic that Malplaquet, too, had been left none the wiser. So now Sebastian explained it again, in plain English. For good measure he threw in Pollock's suggestion that they jam the bridge with a lorry until such time as Fort Pitt furnished the materials to blow it up. Malplaquet listened to this with interest. Nodding approval, he told Sebastian to commandeer a suitable conveyance and park it beside the bridge, ready for immediate use. Then, like Pollock, he withdrew into his Landrover and drove away, leaving Sebastian to put the plan into execution.

Commandeering a lorry, Sebastian learned, was not as easy as it sounded. Even with the Company Commander's authority behind him, he was reluctant to seize one at gunpoint; and those drivers whom he asked politely to hand over their vehicles looked at him as if he was off his head, before accelerating into the middle distance. In the end he made discreet inquiries at the gendarme station and was directed to a small lumber yard near the bridge, whose owner possessed a battered old truck which he could not sell for love or money. The owner was delighted to meet Sebastian. In next to no time they had concluded an agreement whereby Her Majesty's Government would purchase the lorry, provided that the owner or his agents delivered it to a spot nominated by Sebastian, namely the dirt verge on the side of the river nearest Santa Monica. Since the lorry's engine had long ago given up any pretence of functioning, this was achieved by a gang of sweating lumberjacks who manhandled the lorry into position while their employer sat behind the wheel and steered. Smiling broadly, blessing heaven for this providence, he held out his hand for payment. The only official document Sebastian had on him was an army leave pass, so he filled it out in the owner's name and wrote a note promising to pay the bearer the agreed sum on demand at Fort Pitt pay office. He signed the note 'pp M. Pollock'. It had been Pollock's idea, he reasoned. Let him deal with it.

'How long will that lorry stop the Santa Monicans?' asked Willie Hogan, who had followed the war to Mango Creek.

'Long enough. It gives us time to put into effect a mobile defence, if need be, in accordance with a prearranged plan.' By this Sebastian meant that 9 Platoon would run if the tanks broke through.

In fact, though he didn't say so, the same question had been troubling him ever since Pollock had abandoned him to his fate. There was something faintly ludicrous about barring the highway with a broken-down truck. Even a party of dagoes would surely have little trouble getting round it. The subject filled Sebastian with resentment. He had enough to do defending the bridge against Santa Monica without having to defend it against newspapermen as well. Malplaquet had assumed responsibility for the plan – it was his job to argue with Hogan and the other reporters. Not Sebastian's.

Hogan shared a wooden house in Mango Creek with the BBC and a clutch of fellow journalists from Fleet Street. They passed the time playing cards and drinking cheap local rum while they waited for the battle to break. Each lived in fear of one of the others snatching a scoop from under his nose. They watched each other like back-street gossips, becoming highly agitated whenever one of their number was absent for any length of time. It had got so that a man couldn't visit the thunderbox behind the banana trees without being stealthily trailed by his colleagues.

'There is *something* good about it, though,' Hogan told Sebastian. 'It'll look all right on my exes when I send them in.'

'Your exes?'

'My expenses. To accommodation in Mango Creek, £400. To subsistence, the same again. Hire of electric typewriter, say another £100. And Miscellaneous too, that's always a large item. The slut who runs the boarding-house will forge any receipt I ask her.'

'But there's no electricity in Mango Creek.'

'How would Fleet Street know that?'

Day followed day. Before long, 9 Platoon had been there a week. One of the girls from Mango Creek washed and dried Sebastian's jungle greens every morning, so that he could put on a clean pair for dinner when his drummer blew the warning call at five thirty. Partridge served dinner in the ruined house at six sharp. It usually consisted of army compo rations, enriched now and again by a freshly killed jungle fowl. The best the platoon could provide in the way of a cook was Gilligan, who had been given the task in expiation of the fatigues awarded him by Malplaquet. The chickens came to the table with their feet still attached. Sebastian and Sergeant Ball were agreed that Gilligan should be found another job as soon as the invasion scare was over.

Every third day, a helicopter flew overhead and dropped newspapers and bundles of post from home. The newspapers were scrutinised from cover to cover. They were full of drama. From being an obscure item of foreign news, the Casuarina crisis had now advanced on to the lower reaches of the front page. The first report, written the day 9 Platoon left England, carried the headline

AIRLIFT NOT SHOW OF STRENGTH SAY ALLIES
Special to the Washington Post
LONDON

The French battle cruiser Oran *was heading for the Indian Ocean today after unconfirmed reports that Santa Monica was concentrating troops on her border with Casuarina, an Anglo-French island scheduled for independence.*

The Foreign and Commonwealth Office declined comment. The Defense Ministry announced that a battalion of the Gobelin Guards (about 1000 men), together with units of the French army, was flying to the island to carry out 'defense exercises'.

SANTA MONICA

Santa Monica protested the sending of troops to Casuarina, insisting she had no plans to invade the colony.

Sources close to the junta added that last week's devaluation of the escudo had not caused widespread rioting along the border. They denied that troops and tanks had been moved to the area to quell the riots.

Other reports followed. The affair had aroused considerable interest, not only in Washington and western Europe, but also in capitals further to the east. Tass, the official Soviet news agency, seized the opportunity for a tirade against Franco-British imperialism, even though the Kremlin and Santa Monica's junta saw eye to eye on nothing else. The Soviet line was faithfully echoed at Nanterre, where a group of second-year anti-fascists chained themselves to the university railings in a twenty-four-hour vigil against neo-colonialism. *Le Monde* condemned the students but also queried the purity of British motives in the affair, while from London the *Sunday Times* ran a leader article on gunboat diplomacy which summed up the case from every angle and then hinted slyly at French duplicity behind the scenes.

A different slant on the same events appeared in the *Daily Tale*, under the by-line William Hogan.

BATTLING BRITONS HOLD INVADERS AT BAY ran the headline

British troops, entrenched on the refugee-stricken banks of Mango Creek, are poised to repulse imminent invasion by the army of Santa Monica.

Any day now, massed forces will surge across the river in the greatest threat to Casuarina since Vasco da Gama's bearded mariners put the entire population to the sword.

Just 30 men stand between the Santa Monican army and the prize it seeks.

Men like Guardsman Paul Turtle, 18 this week, who asked me to send his love to his mother, Mrs Brenda Turtle, and to thank her for the card – and Guardsman Barry Partridge from Nottingham, who sends all the best to the lads at home.

'You're coming on a bit strong, aren't you?' protested Sebastian. 'Where are all these refugees crowding the river banks?'

'It's human interest,' Hogan replied. He was playing bridge with the other reporters in the room they occupied together. 'We're hot on human interest at the *Tale*. We've got a war of our own, see, a circulation battle with the *Daily Mirror*.' Hogan jerked a thumb at the *Daily Mirror*, who was pouring himself a drink in the corner. 'We're out to destroy the *Mirror* by Christmas. Besides, I have to justify my expenses somehow. If this keeps up, I'll be able to buy a new car when I get home. I've got my eye on a Ford Capri.'

Not long after Hogan's story, a General flew out from England to make an independent assessment of the situation. A very senior General with red on his cap and crossed sabre and baton on his shoulders. He made a whistle-stop tour of the airport, standing sharply upright in the front of a jeep, and pronounced the defences inadequate.

'This battery,' he said, 'will have to be resited. Move it a hundred yards nearer the sea.'

Blending tact with discretion, the Garrison Commander explained that this would ruin a whole series of carefully calculated arcs of fire. He pointed out that the rachet effect would spread around half the airfield, encompassing every trench, every sangar and every almost-completed pillbox.

'Very well,' answered the General. 'They must all be resited. Get the men working on it at once.'

The General was a tough, incisive commander who did not flinch from unpopular decisions. When he had finished with the airport, he boarded a helicopter and flew up-country to visit the front line around Mango Creek. With him travelled an assortment of military acolytes – his ADC, the Garrison Commander, the Gobelin Commanding Officer, the Adjutant, Foxtrot the Intelligence Officer – and, in their own helicopter, two liaison officers from the French contingent, which had finally arrived and was now installed at Fort Pitt. They were met outside the town by Lord Malplaquet, hat in hand, who ran forward to open the General's hatch as soon as the chopper touched down.

Like everyone else, the General was quick to spot the unsoundness of Pollock's strategy for defending the bridge. Followed at a respectful distance by his band of satellites, he strode on to the parapet, looked at the water one side, looked at the water the other, then fixed the Garrison Commander with a gaze that was piercing and blue.

'Whose idea was it to dump that lorry there?' he demanded.

The Garrison Commander looked accusingly at the Gobelin Commanding Officer. The Commanding Officer looked at Malplaquet. Without the hint of a blush, Malplaquet looked at Sebastian. Suddenly Sebastian was the centre of attention.

For one terrible moment the death wish came over him. He debated whether to point a finger at Malplaquet. He was only obeying orders. Malplaquet's was the head that should roll. Instead he said nothing.

'Damn silly,' commented the General.

He stayed two days in the battle zone, living with 9 Platoon and being filmed on the frontier by the BBC, who were covering his tour. He spent the night in a green army caravan which had been driven up from Fort Pitt for the purpose. Gilligan prepared dinner. An attempt was made by the General's entourage to revise the kitchen arrangements in favour of a more elaborate cuisine; but Sebastian – still smarting from the episode on the bridge – saw to it that the high rank were supplied with sausage and beans, the same as everyone else. He was not going to be browbeaten by authority. Nor would he agree to surrender any of the platoon's precious tea ration on demand.

The General, to his credit, knew nothing of this. In private life he was an ascetic man who greatly enjoyed the simple pleasures and resented efforts by his staff to coddle him. Nevertheless, simple life or no, his presence in Mango Creek did nothing to endear him to 9 Platoon. They would have preferred him anywhere but among them. While he was around no one, from the Garrison Commander down to the humblest Guardsman, felt able to relax. He was not welcome. He made everyone stiff and self-conscious, never more so than when they were trapped alone with him in the tactical latrine.

The tactical latrine – tactical because it was held to be within striking distance of the enemy – consisted of a urinal and a camouflaged thunderbox with twin seats. Visiting it after breakfast on the second day, Turtle plumped down without a care in the world and was disconcerted to find himself in silent communion with the General, each with his trousers around his ankles. The older man was unmoved by the experience; not so Turtle. Nobody was more relieved than he when the time came at last to mount a guard of honour for the General's departure.

The General inspected the men, gave them a final word of encouragement, and climbed into the helicopter that was to return him to Fort Pitt. His entourage had already taken their places. Lord Malplaquet closed the hatch from outside, stepped back a few feet and threw up a salute. Sebastian and Sergeant Ball followed suit. The rotors enveloped all three in a swirl of dust as the machine took off in the direction of the coast.

Once airborne, the General relaxed in his seat and unlocked his attaché case. Ahead of him lay an RAF flight to London via Kenya, Cyprus and Paris, where he was to brief the Defence Ministry on the latest developments at the front. Since protocol demanded that he should report first to London, the Paris briefing would have to be off the record. He would deliver it verbally. The written account, the official despatch, would be reserved for his political masters at home. It was to go to Cabinet level. Unscrewing his pen, he began to compose the first draft:

The Minister of Defence
Whitehall
Sir

BRITISH CASUARINA

1 I have the honour to present my report on the above theatre of operations.

2 I found the men in good heart. Morale is high and they are determined to have a crack at the enemy. I have no doubt that they will give a good account of themselves, should it become necessary.

3 The subaltern i/c bridge is keen, but needs watching.

4 I am happy to say that press reports of the refugee problem in Mango Creek have been much exaggerated. I saw no evidence of distress during my tour.

5 *I am less happy about the presence of French troops in the battle zone* (This paragraph was not for consumption in Paris). *At the moment they are being held in reserve, and are convinced that there is a conspiracy afoot to keep them away from the front line. This may prove to be a cause of friction in weeks to come.*

6 *Outlook for the future.* Here the General paused, choosing his words with care. Much depended on the accuracy of his assessment. After due consideration, he wrote *It is my opinion that offensive action by the forces of Santa Monica is not feasible at the present time. I do not believe that the army commanders have any intention to invade. I believe that troop movements along the border have arisen solely in connection with internal disturbances pursuant on the recent fluctuations of the currency.*

The Santa Monicans had too much trouble at home to be contemplating an invasion of their neighbours. The General was convinced of that. Time might prove him wrong, but in his judgement it was all a bluff for domestic consumption. An expensive bluff, as far as Britain and France were concerned, for the movement of troops and missile carriers across the globe did not come cheap. Transport planes as far away as Hong Kong had had to be rerouted to support the operation. He wondered what the final cost would be to the taxpayer. It was certain to be substantial; millions, probably, enough to make a large hole in the defence budget – and to provide political capital for the opposition in Parliament. If he was right, and the Santa Monicans did stay at home, the knives would be out for the army at Westminster. Between one and the other, there would be some explaining to do.

6

The day after the General's departure, the demolition charges arrived in Mango Creek and were wired to the bridge under the supervision of Lieutenant Pollock. Led by a competent-looking Royal Engineers sergeant, the firing party took up residence in its sand-bagged bunker, from which a length of white plastic detonating cord uncoiled towards the supports of the bridge. Across the river, a section of Guardsmen rolled the now obsolete timber wagon off the road and tumbled it down the bank on to the mud flats, where it sank slowly into the ooze. This completed the contingency plan for the defence of Mango Creek.

Although a state of tension existed between Santa Monica and British Casuarina, the timber trade between the two countries had not been suspended. With Sebastian's permission, a lorry from Mango Creek, carrying a full load of wooden planking, set out across the bridge for Santa Monica. He noted the time in his log book as 1200 hours. At 1300 hours he recorded the lorry's return to Mango Creek, still laden with planks. It had been refused entry by Customs on the grounds that its driver had insulted the Santa Monican nation. The cause of the trouble was his road map, which revealed British Casuarina to be a country in its own right. This was heresy to the Santa Monicans, for whom the island was a single nation, one and indivisible. To them Casuarina, French or English, did not exist.

Apart from this incident, the only other distraction of the day was the arrival of the mail helicopter, 9 Platoon's sole visible link with the outside world. It brought news of the home front. Mrs Ball wrote to say that she had been the object of housewifely sympathy at the launderette, where the absence of male clothes in her washing had been interpreted as a sign of divorce. Mrs Gilligan, or rather an anonymous friend of Mrs Gilligan's, wrote to point out that she was seeing more of a rear party lance corporal than she ought. Gilligan seemed unmoved by this, but Sebastian took a note of the details anyway and passed them on to the battalion families officer, who had the thankless task at home of keeping the peace in the married quarters.

As the days melted into one another, and nothing developed, the men began to fidget. By and by, in the continued absence of the enemy, they fell back on their own devices to keep boredom at bay. They vented their frustration by setting fire to the scorpions which infested the ruined building in the belief, erroneous as it turned out, that the creatures would sting themselves to death. When this amusement palled, Partridge arranged tarantula fights between spiders discovered in the surrounding undergrowth. Victorious insects were electrocuted at once with two wires from the radio battery. Other animals were trapped and chopped to pieces with machetes. Now and again the Guardsmen chopped themselves as well, or each other, until gaping wounds and bandaged fingers had become commonplace.

To give the men something less destructive to think about, Sebastian sent to Fort Pitt for a football and set them to work to construct a rudimentary pitch on the open ground beside the planter's house. He organised a five-a-side competition in which everyone, from himself downwards, took part. Games were played in the heat of the afternoon, when the temperature was in the nineties and energy was at its lowest. Although the men complained rebelliously at this, Sebastian knew what he was doing. The non-appearance of the Santa Monicans had left them with a surplus of vitality from which no good would come unless it was effectively tapped. They were looking for trouble, waiting for something to happen, ready, if need be to start something themselves. Under the circumstances, it was only common sense to run them off their feet.

Presently, in spite of Sebastian's efforts, the Guardsmen took to strolling into town of an evening, walking along Regent Street and coming to a stop at the door of a wooden house on which was written *Madame Boongay's Beauty Parlour*.

Soon two of them had venereal disease, of which they were fiercely proud.

Sebastian acted fast. There were few doctors in Casuarina and none at all in Mango Creek. The nearest army doctor was at Fort Pitt, a hundred miles away. He picked up the handset and radioed for advice.

'I'll need blood samples for a Wassermann test,' the medical officer told him. 'I'd rather take them myself, but we're snowed under with similar cases down here. You'll have to do it. I'll send up a medical kit on the next chopper run, plus instructions on how to extract blood. It's quite simple. You just put a tourniquet on the soldier's arm until the vein stands out, then tell him to squeeze his fist. Rub some antiseptic into the crook of his elbow and stick your needle into the vein. When you've got enough blood, put it in a specimen bottle and send it back to me. We'll do the rest this end.'

Sebastian received these instructions without enthusiasm. He did not like the idea, but could see no escape – he had to do what he was told. In a few days the results came back from Fort Pitt. The tests had proved positive and both major strains of VD had been identified. The two sufferers were to report at once to Fort Pitt, where they would receive treatment while the Adjutant debated whether to charge them with administering a self-inflicted wound. The next step, at the Mango Creek end, was for Sebastian to isolate the female carriers and neutralise them before they got to the rest of the platoon.

Once again there was no escape. Sebastian tried to pass the job on to Sergeant Ball, but without success.

'I joined the army to fight,' he said frostily. 'I'll stick a bayonet in a nig-nog, if you say so, sir, but I won't stick a needle in a tart's arse.'

So Sebastian had to do it himself. Leaving Ball in charge of the platoon, he filled a Red Cross satchel with the supplies sent him by the medical officer and tucked the appropriate health manual under his arm. He set off alone for the brothel. Several soldiers offered to point out the way, but he declined their help, preferring that no one else should be involved. Once in Regent Street, he found the place without difficulty and knocked on the door.

It was opened by Mme Boongay herself, owner of the establishment. She was a powerfully built woman of advancing years and mixed racial origin. She had adopted the local custom of wearing curlers during the day and was dressed, appropriately, in a scarlet frock.

'Come in!' she said. She took Sebastian by the hand. 'Come in an' welcome. Sit yourself down. You like a drink? I get you one. What you want to drink?'

'If it's all the same to you, I won't have anything.' Sebastian was feeling nervous. Mme Boongay gave him a friendly pat on the knee.

'Keep calm. Nothin' to worry about! You new here, ain't you? I seen you outside when you diggin' dat hole in de ground, but you never been inside before. I'd have known. Me.'

She was right about the hole. Now she mentioned it, Sebastian realised that this was the house in whose back garden he had built his anti-tank trap.

'I been wonderin' when you comin',' she continued. 'You a friend of Gilligan an' Barry Partridge.'

'In a manner of speaking...' Sebastian would have revealed his errand then, but Mme Boongay had not stopped talking.

'You wanna lay some pipe? Here's what I do. If you like, I got a cherry girl. New in. She cost a bit, mind, but she fresh as de mornin' Jew. Or if you don't want cherry, I got Adelita. She beauty, a real looker, she lay good pipe for a man like you. What you say?'

'Fine. Put them in with the others.' Adelita was not on the list, but it would save time to see all the girls together.

'All of dem? I got a dozen girls here. You want dem all?'

Sebastian explained. 'I'm a ... doctor. I want to examine them. Is there a private room somewhere where we can get together?'

'A *doctor*!' Mme Boongay had misjudged Sebastian. An army doctor was the last person she had been expecting. She was impressed.

Throwing open the door to the veranda, she called at once to her girls, who were sunning themselves on the balcony outside.

'Girls. Come buck-up de new trick. He a doctor. Him here to cure you so, come to make you well.'

To Sebastian's embarrassment, the women on the veranda all stopped what they were doing and turned to stare at him. He was relieved to see that they were fully clothed. Indeed there was little about them to suggest the dubious nature of their calling. They looked like ordinary housewives. There were twelve of them, Creole, Chinese, Indian and negroid; octaroon, quadroon, black and brown; something to suit every taste. Few were pretty, but most were still young. Among them was the cherry girl, twelve years old and – if Sebastian was any judge – already showing the first unmistakable signs of pregnancy.

'De doctor's goin' to inject you, girls,' announced Mme Boongay. 'Make sure now an' get your undies off.'

This they proceeded to do. Unashamedly hitching up their skirts, they gathered round as Sebastian opened his satchel. He took out a syringe and a roll of cotton wool. He had rehearsed the procedure. Keeping his eyes low, he concentrated on filling the syringe with a shot of milky white liquid, the proportions of which were laid down in the handbook in front of him. His audience watched trustfully, not knowing what to expect.

He called the roll according to a list obtained from 9 Platoon. The Guardsmen had made no attempt to discover the girls' real names, but had supplied instead a catalogue of nicknames of their own devising.

'Which one is Mrs Dogend?' he asked, applying a tick to his list as an innocuous-looking Tamil girl ducked her head in acknowledgement. Whiplash Wilma was easily identified by the birthmark disfiguring her face. So were the two sisters A Pack and B Pack, a pair of look-alikes named after the compo rations.

At the rear of the queue, a little apart from the rest, stood the queen of the establishment, Adelita Lemaire. She held herself aloof from the other girls because, as Mme Boongay readily explained, her bust had once featured in an advertisement for a bra. She was small and dark, in her early thirties. Partly French, but with an undeniable touch of negro in her sultry face and a trace of Chinese around the eyes. She had prominent cheekbones and wore her hair long and straight, reaching down the small of her back almost to her waist. She was not beautiful – Mme Boongay had exaggerated – but she was certainly good-looking. In a town like Mango Creek, and elsewhere for that matter, she rated more than a casual glance.

When he had finished, Sebastian put away his syringe and turned to photography. The MO had sent him a Polaroid for the purpose. The girls peeped one by one into the lens. Hooded eyes and pouting lips filled the viewfinder. Without giving any reason, Sebastian took pictures of them all. The photographs were intended to be a deterrent to 9 Platoon, and to any soldiers who might come after. Together with a case history of each subject, they were to be prominently displayed in the platoon latrine, where no one could miss them.

BRITISH TROOPS WIN HEARTS AND MINDS wrote Hogan of the *Tale*. *A battle is going on in Mango Creek for the hearts and minds of the civilians in the front line. A battle fought not with guns and bombs, but with the plastic syringe and the penicillin pack.*

The army's medical officer holds regular surgeries in the town and is making his presence sharply felt.

'We really appreciate what the Guards are doing,' said attractive mother-of-10 Mrs Letitia Boongay. 'They are very welcome here. We all hope they enjoy themselves during their stay.'

To his own mild surprise, Hogan's reporting proved more accurate than he might have guessed.

Word of Sebastian's visit to the brothel quickly got around. Emerging from his sleeping quarters next morning, he saw that the platoon was not alone. Stretched out on the grass were a number of people from Mango Creek, many of them obviously unwell. There were women with shrunken babies in their arms, cripples with twisted limbs and old men complaining of diseases which they could not put into words. The lame, the halt and the blind – all the sick of the town – had found their way up the hill and were squatting patiently in the shade, waiting for the young doctor to appear.

Sebastian was lost for words. Despite the subterfuge with Mme Boongay, he wasn't a medic. These people's problems had nothing to do with him. In any case it was official policy that the locals should not become dependent on army medicine. The answer, according to the book, was to ignore them.

'They won't go away, sir,' reported Sergeant Ball. 'I told them to piss off, but they took no notice. Half of them have never seen a doctor before. They've been saving their complaints for years. It's the chance of a lifetime for the kids.'

'You've *got* to send them away! You know I'm not the MO. Tell them there's nothing I can do for them.'

'They won't believe you, sir. They've heard all about Mme Boongay. They think you're a bleeding miracle. All goodness and light.'

'There's plenty of morphia in the first aid box,' chipped in Partridge. He was enjoying Sebastian's discomfiture. 'And a packet of bandages and the Paludrin tablets. It's the thought that counts – long as they're all given something, they'll go away happy. You can do it, sir, sure you can. You're an officer.'

Sebastian gave him a black look.

'I'll get them sorted into a proper queue,' said Ball. 'Leave it to me, sir. Don't worry about a thing.'

Filling his lungs, he began to organise the mob. 'Women and children on the right, they'll see the doctor first. Old people on the left, they're next. Everyone else in the centre. Come on then. Don't stand about. Move.'

Gilligan was banging the gong for lunch before Sebastian finished surgery. The queue was never-ending. People had come from all over the town with their illnesses and continued to drift in as the sun rose in the sky. Sebastian lanced boils with a sterilised knife, inspected the teeth of little children and listened intelligently to the stomach of an eight-month pregnant Malabar girl. He bandaged stumps and plugged heads. His medical handbooks became greasy with thumbing, his supply of pills steadily dwindled, and still the sick came forward.

Towards the end of the morning, he had had enough. The press of human flesh, the intimate contact of ripe bodies, had taken their toll. He felt drained.

One patient stood out among the few who still remained. A tall unkempt negro with long ragged hair and a knotted beard which grew in dense clumps across his face. Ringlets of woolly matter hung down over the man's eyes and were tossed out of the way with a contemptuous twitch of the neck. His clothes were tattered and torn, patched again and again, but he carried himself without embarrassment. Despite the limp which he was at present affecting, there was a self-confidence in his stride that belied his appearance. He was proud of himself.

Sebastian looked curiously at the negro. The man was a Warlock. He belonged to the Gris Gris movement, a militant part-spiritual part-political brotherhood – originally from Africa – which had established itself by way of dhows and slave ships across the islands of the Indian Ocean. Warlocks believed in magic and salvation from white oppression. Although witchcraft had long ago been banned by the Anglo-French administration, it was still occasionally practised in secret. Its adherents waited now for a sign from their *Bonhomme*, a vision of the supernatural, to deliver them from bondage.

The Warlock had been sitting in camp all morning, waiting his turn in the queue. He raised his arms to Sebastian. 'Bonjour, m'frère,' he said. 'Peace à vous.'

'Peace,' answered Sebastian.

'I is Brother Micah. I see you. I hear you is physician, is healin' de people, givin' out herb to cure de sick.'

Sebastian wasn't going to argue. 'I'm a doctor, yes.'

Brother Micah was in pain. 'I need herb, mon. See here, I got a sickness in de leg. It vex me bad. So bad, now an' now, I no can walk. No can at all.'

Raising his leg, Brother Micah deposited his foot on the table and presented an ankle for inspection. Sebastian and Sergeant Ball looked at it. The ankle was a mass of rags and dirty bandages, tied together with sisal, stained with old blood. They watched without speaking as Micah began to peel off the wrappings.

Despite the patient's protests, however, a closer inspection of the limb revealed more bandage than wound. The packaging disavowed the content. 'It's only a scratch,' said Sergeant Ball. 'A drop of antiseptic'll soon fix that.'

Pouring liquid antiseptic on to a piece of cotton wool, Ball took hold of Brother Micah's foot with his other hand. 'This is going to sting,' he said.

Brother Micah appeared disconcerted through his ringlets. 'Is dat all? What about herb? *Tisane*. You no givin' out herb?'

'Not today, mate.'

'Herb is what I need. It a healin' thing. Herb of de field.'

'Sorry about that.' The bottle of antiseptic was almost empty. Ball made a present of it. 'You bad leg. You take this. You go home,' he said firmly.

Brother Micah saw that no drugs would be forthcoming. Reluctantly he accepted the bottle and a supply of sticking plaster for his ankle. He took his leave without haste. 'Adieu,' he said. 'I goes now. Maybe I see you again, by an' by.'

'Maybe,' said Sebastian.

With a friendly wave, Micah took himself off downhill in the direction of Mango Creek. He had one or two purchases to make in town, and a number of business calls. On the way, he whistled a cheerful tune as he walked. As he whistled, he forgot to limp. By the time he came to Regent Street, out of sight of 9 Platoon, he had begun to walk normally again, as if nothing was the matter with his ankle. Despite its former bloody appearance, no trace remained of his affliction. It seemed that Micah was cured.

'That's my lot for now,' Sebastian told Ball. 'I'm going to get some sleep. If anyone else turns up, give them Paludrin or whatever they want and get rid of them. Make sure you keep them away from me, whatever happens. I've done my bit. I don't want to see anybody.'

It was not to be. No sooner had Sebastian settled into his hammock, snatching a quick catnap, than Sergeant Ball tapped him on the shoulder and pointed towards the battalion Intelligence Officer, who was approaching across a field of debris left by the morning's sick parade.

Sebastian eyed the newcomer warily. Foxtrot was a captain, and regimental custom did not require him to get out of his hammock for a captain. On the other hand, there was nothing to be gained from causing offence, however mild. He got up.

Foxtrot was preparing a situation report on the front line. 'You haven't seen any signs of enemy activity, have you?' he asked. 'No guns, tanks, aircraft, infantry? Nothing I can put in the report?'

'Not a thing.'

'Only I have to check, because it looks as if the Santa Monicans are getting ready to climb down. That's what they think at Fort Pitt, anyway. It seems the invasion business was all a big hoax to frighten the Americans. The Santa Monicans were never serious – the junta has admitted as much, unofficially. What they're really after is money. US dollars. They want the Americans to prop up the *escudo* and keep the country out of Russia's clutches. This sabre-rattling is just their way of saying so.'

'D'you think it'll work?'

'I shouldn't be surprised. The US Treasury has sent in a task force to analyse the currency and decide what's to be done. The Americans are prepared to buy them off. Millions of bucks in foreign aid in return for withdrawing their troops from the border. You can't say fairer than that.'

'Then where does that leave us?'

'No change for the present. We stay here until we find out what's happening. The Yanks have asked us not to stand down for the time being, not until the negotiations have been completed. Till then, we just sit and wait.'

Though he didn't say so, Foxtrot stood to benefit from this development. With luck it would give him time for other things. He was due to sit his A level exam in less than a week. The question papers had already arrived in confidence from England and were locked in the education officer's drawer at Fort Pitt. For Foxtrot, the possibility of attack by Santa Monica had taken second place to the revisionary topic 'How consistent were the aims of the Whig party between 1679 and 1689?' and 'What factors at home and abroad made possible the creation of the Brandenburg-Prussian state by the Great Elector?'

His history notes were kept in his briefcase in a blue folder marked 'Hand of officer only'. For public consumption he was carrying two buff folders, one marked 'Sit rep', the other 'Ganja'. From the ganja file he produced a glossy photo of a tomato plant and laid it on the table.

'It isn't a tomato plant,' he explained. 'It's ganja. It grows wild in the jungle, mostly on the other side of the border. The Indians collect the leaves and crumble them into marijuana. Hashish too — they get that out of the resin from the flowers.'

Sebastian was curious. 'What do they do with it?'

'They compress it into bricks and smuggle it across the river. It goes down to the sea, either on the backs of mules or else hidden in lorries. From there they ship it to America. Florida usually, but New Orleans or Boston as well. It has a high THC content. It gets a good price in the States. That's where we come in. The gendarmes are expecting a big shipment within the next few weeks — there's always a lot of activity at this time of year, after the harvest. They've asked us to keep an eye out for it.'

Foxtrot slid the photograph across the table. 'Pass it round the platoon,' he told Sebastian. 'There's big money involved. If you come across any ganja plants, cut them down and burn them.'

'Will do.' Sebastian studied the picture. More forbidden fruit. It would find a place on the wall of the latrine, along with A and B Pack and the other Polaroid women.

Foxtrot dropped his voice so that the radio operator couldn't hear. 'How are things otherwise? Malplaquet behaving okay?'

'As well as can be expected. I haven't seen much of him, actually.'

This was true. To Sebastian's relief, he had been left largely to his own devices in recent days. The Earl of Malplaquet was preoccupied elsewhere. His headquarters, a pair of tents on a hillside some distance behind Mango Creek, had been invaded by the advance party of a column of Frenchmen who were proposing to dig themselves in across the route to Fort Pitt and the airport. The French troops were lamentably ignorant of their own history. They were genuinely curious as to why their British host should carry as his title the name of a famous French victory. Malplaquet had been diverted by such foolishness from attending the progress of 9 Platoon, and for this Sebastian was grateful. He valued his independence. It was good to have a command of his own, with no one breathing over his shoulder, no one keeping a watch on him. He enjoyed being responsible for his own decisions, free to use his discretion as he thought fit. Long might it continue.

Ironically he had the Santa Monicans to thank for his freedom, for without them he would never have been detached from the rest of Blenheim Company. In Sebastian's book they were a godsend. Whatever else might happen, and despite Foxtrot, it was his personal hope that the crisis would not be resolved for a good while yet – a view shared by Sergeant Ball, and for the same reasons. Neither was in any hurry to go back to regular soldiering; the present arrangement suited them both too well.

7

After he had done his shopping in Mango Creek and paid his business calls, not all of which were well received, Brother Micah made a bundle of his assembled purchases and wrapped them in a hessian sack which he had brought for the purpose. Balancing the bundle over his shoulder, he took the road out of town and set off at a leisurely pace for the interior. He walked for several miles before turning off the track into the jungle, looking both right and left to make sure no one was watching. He was travelling to a very secluded place. It was important that he should not be followed.

Brother Micah was a spy for the Warlock leader Leon Sullivan. He had been sent to Mango Creek to observe the English soldiers who had lately arrived in the town. Certain events were being planned, certain happenings of great moment, which would not benefit from the presence of hostile troops in the vicinity. Brother Micah's job was to weigh up the opposition.

He was a compulsive whistler, and he whistled now as he walked, for his spirits were high. He belonged to the vanguard of an exhilarating revolutionary movement. The day was nigh when the island's *grands blancs*, its European overlords, would be overthrown at last and the true people would inherit the earth. Soon come, soon come! The guns had already been distributed and instruction given in their use. Micah himself was master of an Armalite, which gave his words added weight in discussions around the camp fire at night – and with girls in their huts afterwards. He was looking forward to the day. There was to be a coup, followed by a provisional government. The oppressors would be slaughtered! The island would be renamed New Africa. There would be ownership of the means of production, there would be nationalisation. People would be delivered from every kind of tutelage, in accordance with the law. All this Sullivan had promised. This, and much more. *Aiee!* It made a man feel part of something fine.

A few miles inside the jungle, Micah came by a devious route to the outskirts of the Warlock camp. Putting down his bundle, he beckoned to attract the attention of the lookout. Brother Ton Ton wore reflecting dark glasses and was concealed in the branches of a bois de fer, keeping watch across the forest. Micah treated him with caution. It did not do to creep up on Ton Ton unawares. He carried a submachine gun and had been taught to use it with astonishing speed.

The Warlock camp was a discreet forest glade along the upper reaches of Mango Creek, close to the border with Santa Monica. It was in two parts, divided by a heavy screen of brushwood. In one part dwelled the bulk of the movement, some sixty or seventy Warlocks and their women. In the other part, a short distance upstream, dwelled Leon Sullivan.

Sullivan's dwelling was forbidden territory. It was approached by invitation only, and invitations were rarely, if ever, offered to males. Few men, certainly none of the rank and file, had ever set eyes on his private camp; few women had ever been heard to talk about it.

Sullivan himself, chief *Bonhomme du bois* of the movement, was sitting on a chair in the lower clearing, surrounded by his followers. He wore combat kit and a single decoration, the Order of the Star of Casuarina, amid a display of gold braid.

Brother Micah bowed until his beard almost touched the ground. 'Peace, *Bonhomme*,' he said. 'Whom shall I fear? *Vive le devineur.* Long live…'

'Yes, yes,' Sullivan nodded. 'The soldiers. You saw the soldiers?'

'I seen 'em.'

'How many?'

Micah spread his fingers wide. 'Five hands an' five. One for every day of de month.'

'Thirty, eh. What else did you see? What kind of guns were they carrying?'

'Self-loaders. Every mon got one. An' three machine guns. An' a secret gun which I didn't seen, which dey hide behind sackin', all covered in nets an' tree growth. But I listen hard-ears, I hear talk. It called Carl-Gustav.'

'Anti-tank. It can't do us any harm. What about the other business? The fire prevention tax. I take it you made the calls?'

Brother Micah nodded. Untying his bundle, he rummaged underneath a can of kerosene and produced a wad of bank notes which he had collected on a *pro rata* basis from the shopkeepers of Mango Creek. The money was a form of insurance premium. Shopkeepers who paid it received a guarantee from the Warlock movement that no fires would break out on their property that month. Everyone paid.

Taking the money, Sullivan deducted half for himself and handed the rest to Brother Euclid, waiting at his elbow, whose job it was to safeguard the movement's finances. If Brother Euclid disapproved of the deduction, he made no protest. Sullivan was known to be a wild man with a panga and Euclid was not looking for trouble. Nor did any of the bystanders demur.

Sullivan picked up the kerosene. Brother Micah had used it earlier to encourage the shopkeepers in payment of their premiums. Now it was to serve a different purpose. It was to fuel Sullivan's private fridge, a portable cooler which stood in the corner of his hut, operated by a generator, out of bounds to all save the chief *Bonhomme*. After the revolution, as he never ceased to promise, there would be electricity free for everybody. It would come out of a hole in the wall. Meantime, one had to live as one could.

The fridge contained six bottles of whisky and several dozen of soda. It was Sullivan's one concession to colonial living. Despite his supernatural powers, he found that he always needed a drink at the end of the day. After the revolution, which was not far off, he would be at liberty to leave the jungle and live as he pleased once again. There would be no more outdoor camping, no hardship and privation. He would exist like a human being, in a proper house with a proper roof, with all his creature comforts around him, surrounded by the trappings of success. Until then, his consolation was liquor.

Sullivan had not yet made up his mind where he would settle when the time came. It would certainly be in Europe. Paris possibly, or Gstaad. Somewhere civilised. Somewhere with a high standard of living. Where the women were willing and beautiful, and knew the value of money. A long way from these Warlock buffoons.

Everything depended on money. Until Sullivan took over, the Warlock movement had been grievously undersubscribed. It had needed all his powers of persuasion to organise the brotherhood's finances on to a more stable footing. Kidnapping, extortion, murder – each had played a part. But the most important of all was ganja. The smuggling game was the real money spinner, Sullivan realised; a short cut to immense riches. The American market was booming. US imperialists would smoke all the dope they could lay their hands on. And they paid readily for it, with no questions asked.

Various tried and trusted methods existed for smuggling ganja across the frontier. At first Sullivan had been afraid that the sudden arrival of British soldiers would disrupt his lines of communication, but his fears had proved groundless. A recent dummy run, using a lorry carrying timber, had passed off without incident. The sight of the lorry returning to Casuarina in less than an hour, its load rejected by Santa Monica, had so incensed Customs officials that they had not even bothered to look for the small sack of ganja concealed beneath the wooden shavings.

Now all it needed was one last big load, one final delivery, and Sullivan would be able to retire. The year's crop in Santa Monica was promising to be the richest ever. The ganja had been harvested just before the sinsemilla buds came into bloom and would soon be ready for collection by the Warlocks. They would smuggle it down to the sea, where Sullivan had arranged for the mate of an American freighter to take delivery in return for a down payment of a million dollars, with more to follow. The Warlocks believed that this money would finance the purchase of additional arms and ammunition for the policing of New Africa. Sullivan saw no reason to disillusion them.

He already had plenty of weapons. He had been given them by the Santa Monican government. It was astonishing what one could achieve with a show of initiative. Sullivan had approached the junta with an offer to lead an uprising against the Anglo-French, and the junta had responded with two lorry-loads of small arms and enough equipment to mount a substantial offensive.

Sullivan had had a fright when word first came to him of English soldiers setting up machine-gun nests in Mango Creek. In alarm he had imagined that these troop movements were aimed at him. He had suspected a spy among his own ranks, and had executed two Warlocks on the spot. Later it transpired that the British were expecting to be attacked by Santa Monica – which was absurd when you thought about it, because the Santa Monican army was in no state to attack anybody. Sullivan had been across the border only the other day and had found it in considerable disarray. The blacks were rioting over the price of *posho*, which had doubled in a week, and the army had done nothing about it. Discipline was poor. Some of the troops had thrown away their rifles rather than shoot into the mob.

As long as the Europeans left him alone, Sullivan reflected, nothing could go seriously wrong with his plan. A few more days was all he needed. Collect the ganja, transport it to the coast, and he would be set up for life. Perhaps he would live in both Paris *and* Gstaad. One for summer, one for winter. And women for all the year round.

For the present, though, the charade would have to continue. Sullivan did not believe in the Gris Gris movement any more than he lived in dread of chicken bones or pebbles on a mirror. Money was the only magic he knew. But the pretence had its uses. His followers were all believers, for one thing, and putting the fear of ghosts into them was the best way to keep order in the ranks. Sullivan despised his fellow Warlocks, but he depended on them for a number of reasons, mostly to do with logistics and firepower. Until the big payoff was safely within his grasp, he could not survive without them.

The evening was drawing in. Soon it would be time for whisky and soda, and a pull at the ganja shag. First, however, there would have to be prayers. The Warlocks insisted on saying their prayers every evening, gathering together in a half-circle on the river bank to offer their communal devotion to the shades. It was the high spot of their day, a ritual observed with much ceremony. Though privately contemptuous, Sullivan was always careful to go along with the act.

The men and women had already assembled. Bowing their heads, they joined in the responses as Sullivan led them in evensong, his confident tones uplifted in praise of Africa, extolling the virtues of Gris Gris, bringing down execration on the agents of imperialism. The Warlocks worshipped on cue, devout and solemn. Their faith was unquestioning. For thirty minutes the litany continued, while the sun folded away and the shadows lengthened across the clearing. Sullivan kept watch on his flock from beneath lowered brows. When he judged that the moment was opportune, he made the sign of victory with two dried bones from a black cockerel and held up his hand for silence. 'Cold ground is my bed this night,' he declared. 'Rockstone is my pillow too. Away with the whiteheads! *Mort aux malfaiteurs!*'

'*Mort!*' echoed the congregation.

'Hail to the New Africa!'

'Hail!'

Sullivan held up the bones again. With his other hand he took seven incense leaves and placed them one by one on to a fire made of seven dry twigs. 'We will sing the anthem,' he announced.

The Warlocks raised their heads. At the signal, they burst into song. Their voices were locked together, deep sonorous bass for the men, contralto for the women. The words of the anthem, the last act of invocation, boomed powerfully across the jungle. They were anti-monarchist in flavour:

Allez-vous-en, Elizabeth
Allez-vous-en, mal fée.
Allez-vous-en,

Car maintenant,
La journée grise est arrivée;
Est arrivée,
C'est vrai.

Evensong was over. The anthem died, Sullivan dropped his hands, and the Warlocks slowly turned away in twos and threes towards their huts, where the cooking fires were already beginning to twinkle in anticipation of the evening meal. This was the best part of the day, Sullivan always thought, when the wind blew cool and strong but the ground was still pleasantly warm beneath the feet. A man could sit at ease outside his hut, ice in his glass, catching the breeze while the camp followers argued over who would prepare his food. Sullivan had dozens of followers, and they always argued interminably. Whatever their shortcomings though, the female Warlocks were alert to his every whim, waiting on his every pleasure. It was one of the privileges he would miss when the day came for him to leave the island.

Sullivan had spent some time that afternoon pondering his choice of woman for the night. Eventually, after much deliberation, he had settled on the girl known as Sister Ruth. He had never lain with her before. She had belonged to one of the two spies executed for treachery. But he had always been an admirer of her figure; in particular, of her ample buttocks, which were wide and firm the way a woman's should be. While her lover had been alive, Sullivan had been content to keep his distance, observing the sway of the girl's body and watching her movements surreptitiously from afar. With a rival about, he knew better than to push his luck. Now the lover was dead, however, he meant to possess her without further delay.

Leaning across to Brother Micah, he whispered a short command. Micah nodded. Sullivan watched with bloodshot eyes as Micah sought out the girl and passed on the message from the chief *Bonhomme*. It was an invitation to visit him that night in his quarters.

Sister Ruth forced a smile. She had been afraid of this. She had been expecting it for some time, ever since the premature demise of her lover. In her experience, young women summoned to spend the night with Sullivan in the seclusion of his quarters were often never seen again – particularly if he had been drinking. An excess of alcohol was known to bring out the savage in the Warlock leader. Ruth was downcast. She knew she would have to go – she could not avoid the encounter. But she would not go easily. Sullivan would not have it all his own way, not by any means. Ruth tightened her bra straps for action. She was resolute. She would fight him tooth and claw, ball and fist, to the last of her considerable strength. She would give as good as she got. Then, when all was lost, she would close her mind to the indignity and think only of the fallen lover whom Sullivan had murdered. There was nothing else she could do.

8

Suddenly peace returned to Mango Creek. On the other side of the frontier, the war drums throbbed for the last time and fell defiantly silent. The US Treasury had bought off the opposition. The terms of a loan had been announced whereby the value of the *escudo* would be stabilised in return for a massive influx of dollars from Washington, conditional on the withdrawal of all troops from the border areas. The offer had been accepted in the enemy camp with a great show of distaste. But though the Santa Monican junta remained voluble in the justness of their cause, their display of hostilities was effectively at an end.

These events had no immediate impact upon the garrison of Mango Creek, where Sebastian was carrying out his orders to maintain the soldiers at full alert until further notice. Among civilian observers, on the other hand, it was a different story. No war, no news. The BBC packed up their equipment and chartered the first flight to Nairobi, followed by most of the reporters from Fleet Street. Willie Hogan was one of the handful who remained. Still saving for his new car, he was unwilling to forgo the expenses.

Elsewhere, too, the armed forces began to relax. The *Oran* weighed anchor and sailed northwards on a goodwill tour of Indian Ocean ports. At Fort Pitt, the British and French contingents put on an outward show of normality by reverting to peacetime activities. Sports were organised and a leave roster drawn up. The Gobelin Sergeant-Major sniffed the air and came to the conclusion, in the absence of a strike attack by Santa Monican aircraft, that it would be safe to send to England for his best boots. They arrived by air mail, wrapped in cotton wool and insured for a healthy sum. The same aeroplane brought cricket stumps and a set of pads for the officers' mess. A game was arranged with a native team. It was recorded in the Gobelin Guards scorebook as *Old Etonians vs The World*.

Up-country, the men of 9 Platoon were now free to spend their off-duty hours according to individual preference. When the Drill Sergeant arrived in Mango Creek with the regimental barber in tow, he found them scattered about the town occupying their time as each thought fit. Turtle was sitting naked in the river, reading a war comic. He sat up to his neck in water because it was the only way to escape from sand flies and miniscule no-see-ums. Using the point of his bayonet, Gilligan was carving his initials on the back of a giant tortoise he had spotted near the town. Partridge was at Mme Boongay's, where he had formed a liaison with the sisters A and B Pack, who thought he lived at Buckingham Palace. As long as they had him to themselves, they appeared content to share him – they made no attempt to cut each other out, as English sisters might have done. Instead they spent long hours arm in arm, listening politely while Partridge talked to them about First Division football, a subject on which he was well versed.

Mme Boongay's girls had gone out of their way to make themselves agreeable to 9 Platoon. Whether this was business or pleasure, Sebastian could never be sure. The dividing line between the two was not clear cut. The girls sometimes gave their professional services in return for little golden tins of compo rations. The going rate was a tin of chicken fricassée. Whisper Hungarian goulash in a girl's ear and additional pleasures would be conjured up. Although Sebastian had tried to stabilise the market by removing all foodstuffs under armed guard to the ammunition store, the trade still flourished. For a 24-hour ration pack, the sky was the limit.

One of the few to take no part in this traffic was Turtle. He was fascinated, but aloof. He came to stare, but did not stay to buy. Instead he sat by himself on the veranda of the beauty parlour, prim and self-contained, deaf to the tentative blandishments of the cherry girl, who, for reasons unfathomable, had conceived a fancy for him. He had taken to heart a lecture Sebastian had read the troops on the perils of sex.

'It's clap, sir,' he informed Sebastian smugly. 'Makes you go blind. It ain't worth it, getting your leg over. Not round here. Not unless you know what you're doing.'

At Fort Pitt, now that the emergency was over, Foxtrot had time to take his A Level. A desk had been provided for him in the Education Officer's tent. The Education Officer himself sat on a chair in the corner, reading a magazine and invigilating over half-moon spectacles. He had promised that no word of this venture would escape his lips. Foxtrot had sworn him to secrecy.

With sinking heart Foxtrot surveyed the question paper. *'Discuss the consequences of the invasion of Silesia by Frederick II.'* *Bastard!* The right answer to that lay, in note form, in his briefcase. He had been trying to reach it all week, but the Commanding Officer had kept him fully occupied tying up the loose ends of the Santa Monica affair, and Foxtrot had not been prepared to compromise himself by submitting an unexplained request for study leave. He would just have to answer it blind.

'The consequences of the invasion of Silesia by Frederick II were many and varied,' he began. *'Frederick had been ill-treated by his father as a boy, and was anxious to compensate for this by making Prussia a front-ranking European power. The death of the Austrian emperor Charles VI...'* Charles V? Foxtrot gazed morosely at his fingernails *'... of the Austrian emperor Charles had left Maria Theresa with a large empire and an army weakened and demoralised by the wars of the 1730s...'*

In his command tent, halfway up the hill, the Earl of Malplaquet too had time on his hands. Time, in particular, to review the progress of the campaign, which had begun with such promise only to fail him decisively in his hour of need.

Lord Malplaquet brooded. From his point of view, the Casuarina expedition was not proving to be the success that he had hoped. True, he had not so far made any grave errors of judgement to be held against him in the quest for promotion. But neither had he achieved anything demonstrably in his favour. The way things were at the moment, his chance of making a name for himself, of seizing command of the battalion over the heads of his rivals, was slipping inexorably out of his grasp.

His thoughts turned bleakly to the question of his future. Whatever else might happen, he was determined not to be shuffled over to staff duties; and the image of himself as a civilian was not one that he cared to dwell on. He had made several attempts in recent months to picture himself in the House of Lords, a Conservative spokesman on defence, but the idea had never succeeded in taking root. He was a military man, a soldier, and always would be. He did not belong indoors, in the carpeted corridors of Westminster. He belonged at the head of his regiment.

The battle was not over yet, however. It wasn't lost until it was won. There was still time to retrieve the position, to put himself in good odour with the promotion board – by some means as yet unspecified. The problem as Malplaquet saw it was to persuade the army that he was the right man for the job. Since the opportunity to do so had not so far presented itself, he would just have to create an opportunity of his own. He would make his own luck. He would manufacture an artificial little drama with himself at centre stage, displayed to advantage in the best possible light. The army was ready to be impressed, if he could show good cause. He would find a way.

It was during this flat end-of-term period that the latest in a continuous succession of deputations arrived in Mango Creek from the outside world. The visitors this time were civilians. They occupied a minibus and by their pale skins could be identified as Englishmen newly arrived in the tropics. They called first at the river bank, where they came upon Turtle floating on his back, oblivious to anything but the sunshine. Scarcely bothering to look round, he raised one languid arm in answer to their query and pointed out the direction of Sebastian's headquarters.

The group was headed by a small fleshy man in his late thirties. He wore suède chukka boots and a tight-fitting safari suit of sky-blue trousers and short-sleeved bush jacket, both of which were already beginning to look crumpled in the heat. A gold chain around his neck formed the word BO. When he took off his leather-brimmed hat, it was obvious that he was wearing a toupee of long grey-blond hair.

'He's a handbag, sir, that's what he is,' warned Sergeant Ball.

The newcomer made straight for Sebastian. 'Mr Clinch? Hello! I'm Bo Lindström. You're expecting me.'

'No.'

'You aren't? You should be. Your adjutant told me you'd been warned.'

'The signal must have got lost. Still, now you're here, what can I do for you?'

'It's not what you can do for me, dear boy, it's what I can do for you.' Though his name was Swedish, Lindström's accent was pure Hampstead. 'I'm here to make a film. Really you ought to have been told about this already. I'm a director. I'm making a picture about life in the services, a documentary. It's for the Ministry of Defence. They've hired me to do a recruiting film that they can show in schools and youth clubs. You know the sort of thing: "*Join the army and see the world*".'

'And we're it?'

'You're it. You're the boys in the front line. I've already got footage of the home front – Gunners in Hyde Park, the Edinburgh Tattoo, that sort of thing. What I want now is a good ten minutes of action shots, soldiers doing battle in some unnamed foreign country. Something with spice in it. That's what will lure them into the recruiting offices.'

Delving into the minibus, Lindström re-emerged with a sheaf of papers looped together with string. 'I expect you'd like to see the script,' he said. 'You'll find that it's still very flexible. Plenty of scope for innovation.'

It was not a script so much as a series of storyboards illustrating the progress of a platoon of soldiers travelling by air to a tropical island, where they were instrumental in putting down a rebellion against the government. The climax came in an ambush which annihilated the opposition. Once the dead bodies had been counted, the soldiers took a few days' leave and relaxed on a beach on which palm trees and beautiful women were prominent. Four seconds of an aeroplane in flight then brought them back to England, where the film ended on a swelling note with the observation that it was a man's life in the army – 'and you can learn a trade, too.'

The story was a mirror of 9 Platoon's own experience, from Trooping the Colour – so long ago, now – to active service in Casuarina. Right down to palm trees and women. There was no dialogue. Instead a voiceover traced the evolution of a young man from insipid schoolboy to soldier of the Queen, a path strewn with blood, exotic locations and the unspoken promise of lust among the coconuts. It was a triumph of extrapolation.

To Sebastian's disappointment, Lindström insisted that there was no room for him on screen. The film was not about officers. It was devoted to the other ranks, and to one soldier in particular.

'What I'm looking for is a typical schoolboy,' he explained. 'A soldier with a young face, somebody with whom the audience can identify, so that kids from the slums can look at him and say "This is me".'

'I'll parade the platoon. You can take your choice.'

'Actually I already have one or two ideas of my own. Who was that tall fellow we met in the river on our way here? Youngish looking, rather slender.'

'You can't mean Turtle.'

'Whoever. He had a very interesting face. I should like to see him first. I suspect he may do very well to lead the army into battle.'

Turtle was sent for. He arrived fully dressed, with his hair plastered down, nervous at the unexpected summons. He feared that he had done something wrong down at the river.

Lindström was enthusiastic. 'Yes, yes. A lovely profile. Such cheekbones. He has that perfect *gamin* pinched look. Yes, I can do a lot with those.'

Turtle's eyes swivelled downwards in search of his cheekbones.

'Are you sure?' asked Sebastian. He did not see Turtle as the ideal type the army wished to recruit. 'We do have other soldiers. And there's his voice to consider.'

'No that's all right. The voiceover will be done later by a professional actor. Your man doesn't have to *say* anything. He just has to look right.'

'What about Partridge, for instance? He has a fine physique. He moves very well. Wouldn't he be better?'

'That forehead. Too simian. No, my mind is made up – Turtle it shall be.'

So it was that Turtle became, if not a star, then at least a featured player. It was glory of a kind. In his private fantasies he had always been the man to lead the regiment into battle; now, courtesy of the cinema, his fantasies were coming true. People would boast in pubs that they knew him. Youths from tenement flat and council estate would beat a path to the recruiting office, demanding to be moulded in his image. He had not, to be sure, won the Victoria Cross; but this was the next best thing. Turtle was certain of that.

Filming began next morning. Lindström had planned it carefully. The Guardsmen were to play themselves, patrolling through the jungle; the enemy was portrayed by a band of unemployed negroes from Mango Creek, carrying pangas and wearing green bandannas around their foreheads. Towards the end of their patrol, the Guardsmen would lie in ambush for the men in the bandannas. At the final shoot-out, all the negroes would fall dead.

To begin with, the work went slowly. Early takes were ruined by the appearance in them of Turtle's feet. Under tropical conditions his nailed drill boots had fallen apart and he was wearing civilian shoes – light blue sneakers – until his regulation jungle footwear reached Mango Creek. The effect was distinctly unmilitary, and had made him nervous. 'How do you want me to stand?' was his perpetual refrain. The simplest movement had become an ordeal. Requested to lead the platoon over an open field into a grove of casuarina trees, he advanced unhappily across the ground like a clockwork toy. In the forefront of a river crossing, he plunged into the water with such force that the camera was swamped. The other soldiers were almost as bad. But the director was unperturbed.

'We always get this,' he confided. 'I've got no film in the camera. I'm waiting until they settle down before I start the serious stuff.'

In two hours, as Lindström had predicted, the novelty wore off and Turtle began to unwind. He breathed more easily. By lunchtime he had reverted to his normal self and was striding out manfully as if he had been a patrol commander all his life.

Thereafter, shooting proceeded at a brisk speed. Lindström was on a tight budget. Within three days the patrolling scenes were all in the can, to be assembled later in London. On the fourth morning, at a spot chosen for reasons photogenic rather than tactical, the ambush was scheduled to take place.

Sebastian stood a few yards behind the camera with Lord Malplaquet, who had attached himself to the enterprise in the hope of getting his name on the credits as technical adviser. It was the opening shot in his campaign to win official recognition. Willie Hogan was there too, along with half the population of Mango Creek, fascinated by the process of film making. In front of them the Guardsmen were lying prone along a grassy bank overlooking a path through the scrub. The scene called for the negroes to march down the path, then throw up their hands or clutch their stomachs as the soldiers loosed off at them with blank ammunition. Once the firing had stopped, the soldiers would climb to their feet and advance grimly towards the camera, against a background of coloured smoke.

'But they wouldn't use coloured smoke in real life,' objected Malplaquet. 'Not in an ambush. It doesn't make sense.'

Lindström was patient. 'You won't see the colours on the screen. We're shooting in black and white. The effect will be pure surrealism in the final print.'

Malplaquet snorted. He was not going to surrender his chance of a technical credit without a fight. 'Nonsense. You must be mad. In any case, the Guardsmen wouldn't bunch so close together on that bank.'

'They have to be close to fit into the frame. For film purposes, it's unavoidable.'

'Well, it's inaccurate. The audience will think we're idiots. Where are your stop lines, where are your cut-off men? It doesn't work. If I were you I'd scrub the whole thing and start again. Get it right.'

Lindström gave him a malevolent look. Without speaking, he turned back to the camera.

'Bloody charlie, if you ask me,' said Malplaquet loudly. 'Who is he, anyway? What's he done before? Bo Lindström? Never heard of him.'

'As a matter of fact, some of my previous work has been compared to the best of Schlumberger and Pimperol.'

'Never heard of them, either. Schlumberger and Pimperol! Germans, by the sound of it.' There was triumph in Malplaquet's voice. He felt that he had scored. 'Anyway, what *have* you done before?'

'This and that.' Lindström was evasive. 'Television stuff, mostly.'

Willie Hogan elaborated on this later, when the director was out of earshot. 'Lindström used to work for the BBC. He directed a series for the under-fives called *Peterkin Puppet.*'

'I know it,' said Malplaquet.

But *Peterkin Puppet* was a thing of the past now. Bo Lindström was on his way up. He was waiting for his big break, his chance to show what could be done when funds were generous and cautious hands did not control the purse strings. Until then he was simply marking time. He kept busy with potboilers – deodorant commercials, accountancy training films, road safety advertisements – things he considered unworthy of his talent. One day he would do better. Meantime, he had to pay the rent.

By mid-afternoon the fire fight had been successfully completed. The enemy had walked into the ambush and, with much unnecessary rolling of eyeballs, had fallen to the ground in postures of death. On Lindström's instruction, Sebastian and Sergeant Ball exploded a pair of smoke grenades off-camera. Red and blue smoke billowed into the trees. Turtle strode determinedly towards the lens with a belt of machine gun bullets slung across one shoulder. The effect was impressive. In the background, Malplaquet watched with disapproval.

'That's it,' announced Lindström through a megaphone. 'Right everyone, you can get up now. It's a wrap. That's all I need today.'

As one man the dead negroes came to life and, after a brief consultation, clustered around Lindström. There followed an acrimonious half hour of debate. The corpses demanded compensation for clothing ruined during the ambush. Lindström denied liability and disputed the facts. The corpses became angry. Fists were shaken and voices raised. Malplaquet sided with the blacks. Claim and counter-claim were met with shouting and abuse, but Lindström – an old campaigner – stood firm. He had got what he wanted from the natives. He didn't need them any more.

(A year later, after their return to England, the completed film was shown to the battalion. Sebastian blushed for Turtle. To the sound of dramatic music played *lento* by the band of the Gobelin Guards, the camera zoomed in on a leafy fern which suddenly swung aside to reveal, for the first time, a close-up of Turtle the tracker. His eyes narrowed to slits as he scanned the jungle to left and right of him. 'Many white men pass this way' said his expression. The battalion roared with laughter.)

For the moment, however, the film was not yet complete. The most important part was still to come. The leave scenes were designed to plant in the mind of the viewer an impression of sexual razzle dazzle under a tropical sky. It was necessary that actors and locations for this section of the picture should be chosen with particular care.

'We can't use Mango Creek,' said Lindström. 'It's too awful. Nobody's going to sign on for nine years if they think they'll end up in Mango Creek. I've had a word with your CO. He says we should use the army leave centre on the coast at Englishtown. The budget will run to it. We can stay there quite cheaply. They've got beaches at Englishtown, and buildings made of stone, and neon lights. Neon lights always look good on screen – we can play them up with rumba music and castanets.'

'What about Mango Creek?' objected Sebastian. He was in favour of this plan, but his first duty was to the town. 'Who'll look after the bridge while we're away?'

'Number 7 Platoon will cover for you,' said Malplaquet. 'I shall take command myself.'

'Then there's just one more problem,' said Lindström. Although he and Malplaquet were not speaking to each other, they had tacitly agreed to converse through Sebastian. 'The female lead. There has to be some feminine interest to keep the viewers amused. A woman in a bikini catching a beach ball, maybe. Or else sucking a pineapple through a straw while the soldiers gather round. Someone who looks good. Erotic, but approachable.'

'There are plenty of approachable women in Mango Creek.' Sebastian ran a mental check of the local talent. He could not imagine any of the girls in the town creating a stampede to join the army.

Lindström agreed. 'Our leading lady has got to have screen presence. I saw the most *frightful* woman in Regent Street yesterday. She had a strawberry mark right across her face.'

'Whiplash Wilma. No, you wouldn't want her.'

The image of Wilma touched off a new train of thought. 'There is a woman,' said Sebastian. 'Very good-looking, in fact. Her name's Lemaire, Adelita Lemaire. Her bust was in a magazine once. She might be just what you want.'

'Where can I find her?'

'In town. I can introduce you to her agent.'

Mme Boongay swelled with pride at the idea of Adelita appearing in a movie. She was all smiles. She felt that it reflected credit on her house.

'I always thought dis goin' to happen. Always did. My Adelita, she got appeal. She in a class. No dispute about it.'

Her enthusiasm was shared by Adelita. To the undisguised irritation of the other girls, Adelita at once locked herself in her room on the first floor and dragged out her suitcase from under the bed. After a lengthy toilet, punctuated by much indecision, she slipped into a going-away dress of powder blue, tight around the hips and buttoning provocatively up the front. She put on circular Spanish-style ear-rings which hung down to her bare shoulders, and tied back her hair with a pink ribbon at the nape of the neck. Four-inch heels and a smart shoulder bag, all the treasures of her suitcase, completed the ensemble. When she came downstairs again, Adelita, *poule de luxe*, was the centre of attention.

'You like?' she asked.

Bo Lindström held out his hands in a gesture of appreciation. 'Superb!' he said, and he was right. She looked delightful.

The road to Englishtown led past the garrison lines at Fort Pitt. It was decided that 9 Platoon should spend the night in barracks and set out for the leave centre the following morning. This would give them an opportunity to retrieve their plain clothes from store and change out of uniform for the first time since leaving England.

Fort Pitt was of granite construction and dated from the eighteenth century. Its walls, ten feet thick, had originally been designed to protect French plantation owners from the fury of their slaves. After passing into British hands it had served by turns as powder magazine and prison before assuming its present function of headquarters to the garrison. The flags of Britain and France hung side by side from the yardarm above the main gate, which was flanked by a pair of rusting 4.1-inch guns, souvenirs of a naval action fought offshore during the First World War. Lower down, the flags of the Gobelin Guards and an RAF Harrier squadron shared second billing with the emblem of a regiment of French marines, all of whom were using the fort as a rest camp from the defence of the airport, a dozen miles away.

Inside the walls, the fort boasted two officers' messes – one French, one British – separated by a clothes line and fifty yards of parade ground. By mutual consent, fraternisation between the two compounds did not exist. The British spoke to their French counterparts only on business. The rest of the time they said nothing, but peered darkly across the way from underneath their washing, savouring a rumour that the French entertained coloured women in their quarters after dinner.

The English mess was bordered by a wide veranda containing wicker chairs and back numbers of *The Tatler* and *Country Life*. After the glare of the midday sun outside, the gloom of the ante-room hit Sebastian with blinding suddenness. The mess was crowded. It was the hour of day when garrison officers gathered over a glass of rum punch to read their mail and look at the sports pages before *tiffin*. The twin Colours of the Gobelin Guards, steeped in honours, hung from the dining-room wall opposite the painting of the regiment's Boer War VC. Regimental silver decorated the tables. Yet although this was primarily a Gobelin Guards mess, it was of necessity shared with officers from other branches of the service. The largest contingent came from the RAF. They wore shorts and singlets and occupied one complete side of the ante-room. The other side was held by the Gobelins, properly dressed and loudly critical of these interloping airmen. In the middle, occupying no man's land – and all the copies of *Punch* – sat an uneasy gathering of signallers and gunners who had no place in either camp.

Lieutenant Pollock, the explosives man, belonged to this group. Sebastian noticed that he had been squeezed out to an uncomfortable position midway between the monopoly board and the record player. He was sitting on his own, doing the crossword. As soon as Sebastian came in, however, he jumped up as if stung.

'I want you to look at this,' he said. 'It's my mess bill for last month.'

He thrust forward a creased piece of paper which he had been keeping in his wallet. Sebastian accepted it unwillingly.

MESS BILL. LT M. POLLOCK, RE.

5 × 20	Craven A
6	Planter's Punch
8	Tiger beer
12	Coca Cola
1	Bedford lorry

'What's that lorry doing on my mess bill?' demanded Pollock. 'That's what I'd like to know. I checked back with Colour and he says the Pay Office put it there. It seems some choggy sold the army a lorry and produced a receipt with my name on it. The Pay Office refused to honour the debt out of military funds. They said it was an unauthorised transaction. So they paid him and stuck it on my bill.'

Sebastian played for time. 'I don't know anything about it,' he said. 'It's very odd. Are you sure the lorry ever existed? It sounds like a joke to me.' His eye fell on a Harrier pilot. 'Why don't you try the RAF? They're notorious for that kind of prank.'

He was saved from further discussion by the Colour Sergeant, who announced that lunch was served. The rush for the dining-room was headed by the airmen. There was one large table in the dining-room and two small ones. Though the big table was big enough to accommodate all the officers of the Gobelin Guards, the small one was too small for the RAF. It had become a point of honour to seize the largest table in the name of one's own service.

Lord of all he surveyed in the matter of officers' arrangements was the Adjutant. The Adjutant's role in these surroundings was a nebulous one. In London he exercised tight control over the discipline of the battalion, inspecting uniforms and living quarters for signs of disorder, delivering punishment impartially to junior officers and Guardsmen alike. At Fort Pitt, however, he was beginning to lose sway. Scattered in diverse tents and foxholes, living closer to the jungle than the guardroom, the battalion was no longer within his grasp. Knife-edge creases and polished brass had given way in past months to dull irregular surfaces enabling the wearer to harmonise with a foliate backdrop. Even the parade ground, God's half acre, had become a depository for stubbed-out Gauloises. It made the Adjutant feel redundant.

What upset him more than anything, more even than the French, was the RAF. The pilots of the RAF were men of undeniable technical accomplishment, but low social standing. Like Pollock, they combed their hair forward – sometimes in public. Like Pollock, they were entitled to sit in the mess. Out of uniform they wore football shorts and vests from Marks and Spencer. They called each other 'mate'. Sometimes they ordered brown ale in bottles and said 'cheers' when they drank it. The Adjutant despised them. He made his feelings clear by denying them his conversation. The RAF did not notice. He despised them still more.

Matters had recently come to a head. It had been agreed between the two services that officers should dress for dinner in Planters' Order – a regimental tie and a plain clothes shirt with crested cufflinks at the wrist. But nothing would persuade the RAF to dress uncomfortably at any other time of day. They persisted in wearing soccer strip during the afternoon. Now and again they came indoors in sneakers. The Adjutant retaliated by causing a large notice to be posted in prominent type. The notice was short and sharp. *Gentlemen of the Gobelin Guards*, it said. *Both upper and lower parts of the body are to be covered in the mess.*

If this was meant to be a rebuke to the junior service, it did not succeed. The pilots were unimpressed. They said nothing, but sat in their vests and rocked with mirth behind their newspapers. One evening, after they had had too much to drink, they hid the Adjutant's bed in the swimming pool.

It was the final straw. 'Such a pity the Few never get any fewer,' declared the Adjutant. 'They're all the same, that's their trouble. Oiks! No idea how to behave.'

'Oh I say! Eton, Sandhurst and the Guards! Do have another ginger biccie!'

'To hell with Eton.' The Adjutant had failed the Common Entrance to Eton and was known to be sensitive about it. His riposte was swift. 'Besides – where were you at Waterloo?'

In his world, there could be no answer to that.

9

Leon Sullivan sat in the jungle drinking Black Label and counting his shrunken heads, which were suspended in a row from a wooden rail outside his hut. He had so many, it was becoming difficult to keep track. Each one was a memory, an incident from his past, a reminder of good times and happy bygone days. Sometimes a love affair, sometimes a quarrel, once a challenge to his leadership. The two Warlocks executed for treachery were there, along with many others, most of them old friends. The majority of the heads on the rail had been close to him at some time, had known him well and would be with him now for the rest of his days, eyes hooded, nostrils sewn up, mouths aghast in expressions of permanent dismay.

Sullivan was a skilful headshrinker. It was a trick he had learned from the maroons in the interior. You made a slit in the back of the neck and drew out the skull in one deft movement, like turning a grapefruit inside out. Then you filled the aperture with hot stones, until the hissing sizzling flesh had contracted to the size of a monkey's brain, not more than four inches across. It was a simple operation. Easier than frying bacon.

The heads were a photograph album for Sullivan, a scrapbook of his past life. He never tired of their company. Drinking with them, he had found, was more pleasant than drinking alone. He lifted his glass in a toast. 'Here's luck,' he told them.

Across the camp fire, he shared the gossip of the day. The heads listened sagely as Sullivan told of strange goings on in Mango Creek, whence Brother Micah had just returned from working as an extra on a film of unexplained significance. The film had involved a mock battle between Warlocks and the forces of capitalism. An omen for the future? Brother Micah reported that the Europeans had been issued with bullets which had no impact when fired, that the machine guns had sputtered harmlessly into the void. Sullivan realised the soldiers had been firing blanks. But what were they doing loosing off clouds of smoke? – all colours of the rainbow, according to Micah, whose description of the events had been vivid. The way Micah told it, it sounded more like a carnival than a serious military operation. An odd business and no mistake. Sullivan could not fathom it out at all.

He got up and walked over to the fridge to replenish his glass. The light came on inside as he opened the door. It revealed the severed head of Sister Ruth in the top compartment, packed in crushed ice, staring at him in tones of glacial astonishment.

Sullivan regarded the head affectionately. What a struggle she had put up! His body was still raw all over. She had kicked and bitten and fought until he thought she would never surrender. She had scratched and squawked until he had had to knock her half-senseless. A great woman. Plenty of spirit. He would remember her for a long time to come – even, in the sober light of day, with a tinge of regret. It had been almost a shame to use the strangling wire on so vibrant a being, to cut off the head and separate it from those young shoulders. Almost a shame. Girls like Ruth were few and far between.

Her body was still lying where he had left it, on the river bank, covered in blood and dust and swarms of sated flies. Both fists were tightly clenched, for Ruth had not died easily. She had taken a mass of punishment before she succumbed. After a day in the sun, rank and putrid, her body was a forlorn, grotesque sight, an affront to human dignity. It was ugly and repellant. It also smelled bad.

Sullivan wrinkled his nose in distaste. Pooh, it would have to go. Putting down his drink, he took hold of Ruth's ankles and dragged her naked corpse towards the river. The flies rose in disarray. Sullivan placed his foot against the small of Ruth's back and pushed hard. The body flopped forward and splashed obscenely into the river. In a whirl of arms and legs it disappeared below the surface and sank at once to the bottom, scattering the catfish which had been lazing in the shade of the reeds among the shallows.

Satisfied, Sullivan dusted off his hands. That was that. The current would soon wash Ruth away. The place was smelling better already. Kneeling down, he spat delicately on to one of the stones he had put on the fire and watched the spittle evaporate. The stones were heating up nicely. Soon Sister Ruth's head would join that of her ex-lover on the rail beside the hut.

The rest of Ruth spent some time on the bottom of the river and then rose swollen and bloated to the surface. She floated aimlessly for a while, drifting this way and that, before the undertow caught her and carried her off stiff-legged downstream. From bank to bank she made erratic progress, borne along on the stream like a piece of majestic driftwood, until the sluggish waters broadened and deepened into the wider expanse of river that marked the township of Mango Creek. Here, eddying and swirling, she rolled over twice in front of the fascinated washerwomen lining the shore and came gently to rest, as a harbouring dreadnought, against one of the stanchions of the bridge.

Foxtrot and Lord Malplaquet went down to watch the police fish her out. Willie Hogan was there already, taking photographs. The three of them stood upwind and held handkerchiefs to their faces as a party of gendarmes passed a rope around the corpse and hauled it ashore. The smell by now was tremendous.

Foxtrot was impressed by the body. He was in Mango Creek to monitor the ceasefire, but a headless corpse was something else.

'Look at those bruises!' he declared. 'They're all over. Whoever did it must have cut off the head to prevent identification.'

'It's a woman, though,' said Malplaquet.

'Definitely a woman.'

The gendarme sergeant in charge of the case was a cheerful man, undismayed by the presence of death at his feet. He cast a professional eye over the corpse and knew immediately who was responsible. Leon Sullivan always left his trademark. His teeth had become a byword in the force. Holding his nose, the gendarme sergeant turned the body over and made a careful study of the buttocks. Yes, there they were, a complete set of denture prints embedded in the flesh. Teethmarks all over the bum. There was an unqualified dentist in Mango Creek, a refugee from Maputo, who had once taken a record of Sullivan's teeth. He would be able to identify them. But the sergeant knew he would have to hurry. If he left it much longer, the body would have decomposed before he had a chance to get a plaster cast made.

He gave Foxtrot a gap-toothed grin. 'Is good,' he declared.

'I should say so,' said Foxtrot.

10

Englishtown, scene of Bo Lindström's location shooting, was the capital city – indeed the only city – of British Casuarina. It was a small natural harbour on the south coast, bordered by trim beaches of sand and shimmering palm. Its original inhabitants had been Arabs, a heritage reflected in the decor of the many bars and night clubs attached to the hotels along the tourist strip. The tourists themselves, mostly British and French, had stayed away in great numbers during the invasion crisis. Now they were beginning to return, in ones and twos at first, and then by the planeload as the charter companies resumed service from London and Paris.

Away from the tourist strip, the town was an unpleasant conglomeration of tin shanties and wooden houses raised on stilts to catch the breeze from the ocean. The shanties were built of tar paper and corrugated iron, or beaten out oil drums, held together with chicken wire. Stone buildings were not as numerous as Lindström had been led to expect. The few that existed were built in the French colonial style, with deep verandas on every floor and ornate façades of crumbling plasterwork, from behind which the ladies of the town could watch the goings-on in the street. Points of interest were equally scarce. All that met the eye were the Vasco da Gama monument, the cricket ground and a severe-looking statue of Queen Victoria on a pedestal in the Place d'Austerlitz.

The army's leave centre, where 9 Platoon were staying, was a modest pension in a side street, the other end of town from the big hotels. It was plain and unpretentious, consisting only of a number of simple bedrooms grouped around a central courtyard open to the sky. The owner had undertaken to provide bed and breakfast for the platoon and film crew, at a price the soldiers could afford. Beyond that, they were on their own.

Bo Lindström had been sullen and dispirited during the tedious coach journey from Fort Pitt, but came to himself again after a few hours' respite at the pension. A siesta and a change of clothes put new life into him. Soon he and his cameraman were out on the streets with a light meter, exploring the mouldering architecture and brightly-hued shanties of the neighbourhood. They spent all afternoon wandering up and down, scouting locations and taking note of possible camera angles, seeking a festive choice of backdrops for the soldiers' holiday. Their researches met with success. Whatever its other failings, the town was packed with life and colour; it was ideal for their purpose.

Work began soon after dawn next day, when Lindström swept the platoon off to the city centre to photograph them wandering around the old slave market before a crowd had a chance to gather. In this he was hardly successful. Although the camera was set up inconspicuously behind a basketseller's barrow, the residents of Englishtown were not easily duped. Even the hostile presence of Sergeant Ball did not discourage them from peering into the lens in the mistaken belief that their friends and relations would see them the other end. According to the script, Turtle was supposed to negotiate the purchase of a polished tortoise shell, while Adelita rested one hand in admiration on his shoulder. But the owner of the shell was more interested in the camera across the street than the business in hand. So were the gesticulating townspeople surrounding the film unit. Lindström attempted the scene three times. Then he abandoned it and retired to his room to flip through *Unknown masters of Japanese cinema* until such time as the world should come to its senses.

Later, after he had been coaxed from his bed, an attempt to photograph Adelita and Turtle embarking on a joy ride in a tourist rickshaw proved more successful. Lindström filmed the scene from the safety of the hired bus which had brought them from Fort Pitt. The rear window was too high for onlookers to intrude. Hand in hand with Adelita, Turtle mounted the step with a fixed grin and ordered the rickshaw boy to drive on. The vehicle sagged visibly as he folded his bulk inside. 'Look as if you're enjoying yourself!' yelled Lindström through the window. 'Ha, ha!' chuckled Turtle obediently. The rickshaw boy tugged at the shafts; bus and ghari moved away from the kerb together. It was a wrap in one.

This left only a grand finale on the beach. For his swan song Lindström had chosen a secluded cove about ten miles west of the city, beyond the orbit of the large hotels. The platoon packed swimming trunks and a crate of beer and travelled by coach in excellent humour. While Lindström fussed over the camera, Partridge and Sergeant Ball organised a game of football on the sand. Except for the soldiers, the beach was deserted. Turtle, as centre forward, had the ball to himself. Because his body had seen little sun below the waist, his knees had been painted with make-up to match his arms. He put on as fancy a display of footwork as his odd-sized feet would allow, twisting first one way and then another, kicking up spurts of sand and playing the ball around his opponents, who made little effort to stop him. The camera rolled, the soldiers laughed. The sea was blue and Lindström was happy.

Adelita, meanwhile, had emerged from behind the coach, where she had been changing her clothes in preparation for the final scene, featuring herself and Turtle. They were scheduled to run through the surf and relax together in the shallows. Adelita was wearing a modest white bikini. It revealed a figure which, for grace and simplicity, would have earned the unequivocal hatred of smart women in London or New York. Her hair was pinned behind one ear with a scarlet flower. She was almost beautiful, and knew it. Although her smile was sweet, it was obvious to Sebastian that her eyes glittered with cold calculation.

Businesslike, Lindström took her elbow. 'Come along, my dear, you hold hands with Turtle. That's right. There's a good girl. Now wave to the camera with your other hand, turn your head towards it… Smile … that's good, that's good. Lovely!'

Sebastian lost count of the number of times Turtle and Adelita bounded across the beach and plopped down in the glistening foam with their arms around each other's necks. Whatever they did, Lindström was not satisfied. For this scene he demanded perfection. He tried it several different ways, shooting from shore and from sea (the cameraman up to his waist in water), using a variety of backgrounds, before he found the right answer. The two players performed with a will. After perhaps a dozen takes, it began to fall into place. By now Turtle was covered in sweat, but had lost none of his initial enthusiasm. He nestled close to Adelita. Something akin to passion heightened his embrace. It must have looked good on film, because Lindström clapped his hands and lifted his hat to the pair of them. The cameraman was pleased, too. The final scene was in the can. There was nothing more to be done.

That evening, Lindström took Sebastian and Sergeant Ball to a night club for a farewell party. Tomorrow he was going back to England, but tonight he would celebrate. He reserved a table for three at the Chinese Disco. According to the placard in the foyer, it was Englishtown's 'hottest nite spot'.

Strobe lights flickered as the three men sat down. There was no one to take their order. Instead a Portuguese Creole in a full-length *kitenge* dress made her way through the crush and joined them uninvited.

'My name is Marie-Carmen. I will sit with you.'

Lindström eyed her with distaste. 'Not for me, dear. Try one of the boys.'

'Yeah, go on,' said Ball. 'No harm in it. What'll you have, love?'

'I have champagne. I will order a bottle.'

'Half a minute,' cautioned Sebastian. 'Who asked for champagne? Rum and coke will do me.'

'Gin and It,' said Lindström.

'Mine's a pint,' said Ball. 'They must sell beer here.'

'No beer. Is a night club. No beer.' Marie-Carmen shrugged.

'Rum and coke, then.'

They waited for the drinks to arrive. When they came, there were four cocktail sticks in Marie-Carmen's glass, none in any of the others. She was drinking coloured water.

For a hostess she was not particularly good-looking, but neither was she unattractive. She looked like a shop girl, plump and placid. With skill born of long practice she bummed a cigarette from Sergeant Ball and bowed her head as he lit a match. Then she leaned back and blew a smoke ring towards the ceiling. Though her body was sitting at the table, her thoughts were obviously elsewhere.

'You are South African?' she asked.

'No,' answered Sebastian.

'No?'

'Emphatically not. British.'

'Ah, British.' Having settled that question, Marie-Carmen leaned back in her chair once again and tapped her foot in time to the music. She waited a while before trying once more. 'You like marijuana? Ganja? You like to buy? I know a man who can sell you the best. Low price, top quality – any kind you want.'

'Not for us, thanks. But we'll have another round.'

They ordered the same again. Another four cocktail sticks were delivered to Marie-Carmen. She fished them out of her glass and locked them in her handbag with the first four.

'Down the hatch,' said Ball.

Marie-Carmen examined her nails. The disc jockey put on 'Sun of Jamaica' and turned up the volume. The noise was deafening. Looking across the table, Marie-Carmen shouted at Sebastian: 'You like to dance?'

'Not if I can help it. Try my friend here. He's a dancing man.'

Ball emptied his glass and stood up. He edged around the table and led Marie-Carmen to the floor. Soon they were out of sight among the writhing bodies.

'Wretched female,' said Lindström. He finished his gin and called for another. There were holes in the shoes of the waiter who brought it. 'What time does the floor show start?' he asked.

'Soon come.'

'Is it good?'

'Bien sur, mon. Uh huh.'

Ball and Marie-Carmen returned to the table. The girl took the chair next to Sebastian. Their forearms touched as she sat down. Sebastian noticed that her legs were quite shapely underneath her dress. By his reckoning there were now sixteen cocktail sticks in her handbag – or was it twenty? Whatever the score, the drink was beginning to take effect. A combination of noise, alcohol and dim lighting had got into the bloodstream. He felt fine, better than he had felt for a long time. So did Ball. Calling for more drinks, they loosened their collars and settled in for a lengthy session. To no one's surprise, Marie-Carmen remained sober. But Bo Lindström did not.

'I don't know why I'm in this business, I really don't,' he confided, twirling the stem of his glass.

'What business is that?' Ball, normally suspicious of Lindström, was interested.

'The movies. Moving pictures. The visual arts.' He snorted. '*Visual arts*! You should tell that to the people I have to work with.'

'What's wrong with them?'

'What's right? Second rate, that's what they are. Deadbeats. No talent. Just in it for the money.'

'They've got to eat.'

'Eat! That's all some people think about!' Lindström thumped the table. 'Does Schlumberger eat? Does Pimperol? Thin as a stick, both of them. Glorious figures.'

'Speaking of foreigners,' interrupted Sebastian, 'there's something that's been bothering me about you. Your name. Why have you got a Swedish name? You sound distinctly English to me.'

'And so I am, dear boy. It's a *ruse de guerre*. You'll find that all of us in the film business are adopting foreign names nowadays. It's that or writing dialogue.' He became conspiratorial. 'Promise you won't tell a soul, but my real name is Lillipuss, Ben Lillipus. Imagine!'

'What about Schlumberger and Pimperol? Are they English too?' Like the Earl of Malplaquet, Sebastian had to confess that he had never heard of either.

'Of course. They're from Clapham. In fact they used to share a house. But Schlumberger made his name before Pimperol and they haven't spoken a word to each other since.'

'What are they famous for?'

'A blend of film noir urban nightmare and Bressonian formalism. It shows in all their work.'

Lindström drew closer. 'And I'll tell you something else you don't know. This isn't the first time I've worked on a film with a guardsman. No way! Not by a long chalk!' He lowered his voice. 'You want to know when I worked with a guardsman before? I'll tell you. It was when I first went freelance. Underground cinema. He was in the Coldstream Guards – an enormous lad. I met him in a pub behind Wellington Barracks. He wore a cat mask on screen to protect his identity. We shot the film in one day. You probably haven't seen it. *Poofter in boots*, it was called.' Lindström giggled. 'Naughty Ben! I shouldn't have told you that.'

'Nao entendo *poofter*,' said Marie-Carmen.

The door to the street opened and three figures lurched in. Through the gloom Sebastian recognised two of them as Partridge and Turtle, dressed in plain clothes. Partridge was nursing a black eye, outcome of a brawl with the French army. His wardrobe had not changed at all from Chelsea coffee bar to tropical night club. He wore bovver boots and braces over a thick check shirt buttoned, in accordance with walking-out regulations, at the wrist. Turtle had been more imaginative. His new-found status as film actor had gone to his head. He had blossomed into a multi-coloured beach shirt and an immense straw hat, almost as wide as his shoulders, tied with string underneath the chin. The first diffident sprouting of a moustache was visible on his lip. Tucked under one arm, restricting his movement, was a souvenir *moutia* drum of vast dimensions. He was wearing dark glasses and smoking a cigar.

Beaming drunkenly, he put down the drum and shook his drumsticks at Sebastian. 'Good, aren't they, sir? Got 'em down the market.'

He was leading Adelita with his other hand. She and Marie-Carmen gave each other the once over and turned their heads away.

'What'll you have, sir?' asked Turtle expansively. He was buying drinks. 'Let me get you a beer.'

'They don't sell it. And the prices are ruinous anyway. I'll just have a coke.'

'No beer?' Turtle was incredulous. 'No beer? What are you talking about?'

'No beer. A coke'll be fine.' Sebastian was anxious about Turtle's pocket.

But Turtle was not to be dissuaded. He was authoritative. He badly wanted to impress Adelita. 'You just leave it to me, sir,' he said sweatily. 'Let me handle it. I'll get you a beer. Don't you worry. No trouble.'

Clicking his fingers, he peered round for a waiter. None came. Instead, a change swept suddenly over his features. Abandoning the attempt to impress Adelita, he staggered outside to be sick.

'He never should have had that cigar,' said Partridge.

A gaggle of dancing girls in native costume appeared on stage. The floor show was about to start. As the lights went down in the house, Marie-Carmen rested a hand on Sebastian's knee and he was glad of it.

The show was poor. Pap for the tourists. It was crude and unimaginative. Underneath the table, Sebastian held hands with Marie-Carmen; Ball and Lindström were engrossed in the music. They lingered until the end, in the faint hope of seeing the girls take their clothes off, but were disappointed. When the lights went up again, Lindström called for the bill.

'Come home with me,' whispered Marie-Carmen. She put the tip of her tongue in Sebastian's ear.

'I can't,' he said. 'It's not that I wouldn't like to, but I can't.'

'Come to bed. Very nice, very clean.'

'I'm sorry.'

'I think she fancies you,' said Ball.

'Plenty money, plenty honey. I live close. I am very clean. Come with me.'

'Some other time.' Regretfully, Sebastian rose to go. Marie-Carmen did not seem as put out as he would have liked. She made no attempt to argue. He patted her rump and gave her a large tip which disappeared immediately into her purse. They said goodbye. She left them and headed for the bar to cash in her cocktail sticks. Sebastian watched her out of sight, strongly resisting the urge to follow.

Sergeant Ball began to collect bodies for the return trip to the pension. The situation was confused. Turtle, white-faced and limp, didn't know where he was and would have to be escorted by Adelita. Partridge was insisting he could manage on his own. Bo Lindström, lost in self-pity, had decided not to co-operate – he did not want to share a taxi with the others, but declared his intention of taking one on his own, regardless of the expense.

Sebastian was still thinking about Marie-Carmen. He cursed himself for a fool. She was no beauty, certainly, but she was scented and wholesome and appeared in blatant good health. He could have done much worse. The opportunity did not present itself very often and he had fluffed it. He had allowed the army's VD film to scare him off. A terrifying scenario of scabs and blindness had done its work ('You'll never play football for the battalion again' had been the grim warning in the film). What an idiot he was. Nothing would happen if he was careful. Sebastian hesitated on the pavement outside the disco, torn between passion and prudence, lust and caution. He peered indoors, hoping for a sign, but saw none. Marie-Carmen had disappeared. With an effort, he tore himself away and followed the others into the taxicab, home to a chaste and lonely bed. It seemed such a waste. He wasn't in the football team anyway.

Remorse, remorse! A subdued platoon of soldiers shrinking from daylight next morning, scattered in disorder across the seats of the coach delivering them back to the army. A hangover for Turtle; bags under the eyes for Lindström; the nagging thought for Sebastian, the certainty, that he had missed out on Marie-Carmen. Even a slight dullness in the head for Partridge and Sergeant Ball. Remorse among all ranks – profound, regretful and sincere.

It was Bo Lindström's – Ben Lillipuss's – last morning in Casuarina. He and his camera crew were scheduled to return to England on the weekly RAF flight from the international airport. Not before time. They had been counting the days.

The plane had delayed take-off against the coach's arrival. It stood waiting on the runway beside the terminal building, while ground crew milled around it with chocks and fuel bowsers. A flight sergeant was checking his watch in the departure lounge. Lindström's men carried their own bags out to the aircraft and handed them up to the luggage bay. The cameraman fought off attempts to relieve him of his precious reels of film and kept them under his arm, where they would be safe. He could not afford to lose them. He did not want to have to come back to British Casuarina if he could avoid it.

'Farewell Sebastian, *mon brave*,' said Lindström. 'The boys in blue will be taking care of me from now on. I can't pretend I'm sorry to leave.' He waggled his fingers at the platoon. 'Come and see me if you're ever in London.'

If they were ever in London! The platoon winced. Lindström was being unkinder than he knew. The men had begun to wonder when they would see England again, if the day would come when a silver bird would waft them skywards and homewards, as it was now wafting the film crew. They had their doubts. For them, as for Lindström, the Indian Ocean had long since lost its appeal. They watched in silence as the big Hercules thundered down the runway and took off over the sea, gaining height steadily on the first leg of its long haul back to civilisation. Their thoughts went with it in wistful profusion. England was writ large on their faces. They were thinking of frost and television and running water; of clean sheets and football; of tube trains, shop fronts and drizzle; of autumn leaves and whether they would be home for Christmas. Lindström's departure made them uneasy. They, too, wanted to go home.

They were brought back to earth by Foxtrot. He was waiting to brief Sebastian on what had happened at Mango Creek while the platoon had been away. He began with a mugshot of an unpleasant-looking negro, who by his appearance was obviously a Warlock.

'Leon Sullivan,' he explained. 'Chief *Bonhomme du bois* – witch doctor – of the Gris Gris movement. Poses as a spiritual leader, the man who will lead his flock out of bondage, but is really a businessman aiming to make a fortune from drugs and allied activities. Protection rackets, extortion – all the usual things. He's a big time gunman, no proven criminal record, only recently come into prominence. I've made some inquiries and nothing is known about him until a year ago, when he first got involved in Warlocks and drug-running. Since then he's done a great deal. He's been in touch with the Santa Monican government, and he's trained his hardcore Warlocks – about sixty of them – into quite an efficient little fighting force. Quite efficient. Where he got the expertise I can't imagine. Russia probably, or Cuba. He can hardly have learned it from the Santa Monicans.'

'Where is he now?'

'In the jungle somewhere. He's wanted on a murder charge. He killed a woman about ten days ago and left incriminating evidence on the body. The gendarmes have just identified it. They're certain he's their man.'

Sebastian studied the photo of Sullivan. The eyes were hooded and supercilious, the nose flat and broad. His hair hung down over his face in frizzy twists, obscuring his ears. He wore a beard. He looked to be about thirty.

'You know it's a funny thing,' Sebastian said, 'but I could swear I've seen this man before somewhere. Something about his face is very familiar. I don't know what, but I'm sure I recognise him.'

Sebastian laid the photo out flat and put his thumb across the top half of the forehead, covering the hair, so that just the man's face was visible. It was an old trick, but it did not work. With his other thumb Sebastian covered the beard until only the man's eyes and nose remained. Still no luck.

'I've seen him before,' he insisted. 'I'm certain of it.'

'They all look alike to me,' said Foxtrot. 'Anyway, if you see him again, you know what to do. Pick him up if you can, otherwise get the police on to it. But whatever you do, be careful. He's armed and dangerous. He wouldn't hesitate to fight his way out of trouble if he had to – and if the body of that woman was anything to go by, he could cut up pretty nasty.'

As soon as Foxtrot had gone, Sebastian took out Sullivan's picture and looked at it again. Somewhere, sometime, he had seen that face before. Not in Mango Creek, because he would have remembered it. Somewhere else. He had no idea where. For the life of him, he could not imagine how their paths might have crossed.

11

Malcolm Pollock was a man who brooded and counted pence. The sort of man to whom one Bedford lorry more or less made an appreciable difference. He was a connoisseur of mess bills, a scrutiniser and itemiser of accounts down to the last detail. He revelled in paperwork. During his time at Sandhurst he had thought seriously of joining the Royal Army Pay Corps, and had only been dissuaded by the promise of a fleet of bulldozers to call his own if he pledged himself to the Engineers. But his love of paperwork remained. The arrival of his mess bill was often the highlight of his month. Pollock had never forgotten the time the garrison wine waiter charged him for a packet of Craven A on a day when Pollock was deep in the jungle mending roads. Nor had the wine waiter. The resulting inquiry turned up a nest of vipers in the mess accounts, and the man had been sentenced to six months in Colchester. He was still doing his time.

But the case of the Bedford lorry was something different. There was no question of corruption in the accounts, nor even of a mistake. No one had erred. The entry was as plain as anything. Pollock had the supporting documents in front of him. An army leave pass – strange, that – made out as a bill of sale, the details scrupulously entered in black ink, all legal and above board. Everything was as it should be, neat and precise, except his own signature in an alien hand. It was most odd.

One thing was certain, though – Pollock was not going to pay for the lorry if he could help it. He had volunteered for two years in Casuarina to save money, not spend it. Life in a tropical mess was very cheap. By spending little and hoarding his local overseas allowance, Pollock could be certain of a tidy nest egg to await him on his return home. He was putting money by for a new motor car. He could see it already in his mind's eye, a new-registration Mini Metro, straight from the showroom, a fitting example of fuel economy and mileage per gallon. He had picked out the model in motoring magazines his parents sent from home.

Pollock was an enthusiast. He inhabited a world of wheelbases and camshafts, of cylinders, halogen lamps and Christmas presents that came in steering wheel shapes. Though he hadn't yet put the money down, his new car was almost saved for; the rewards of planning and thrift would soon be his. He was not going to be robbed of his prize by foul play.

What to do? Pollock took off his spectacles and polished them. The answer was to track down the culprit and confront him with his guilt. But how? The evidence, to say the least, was slender. All Pollock had to go on was the identity of the person who had sold the truck to the army. According to the Pay Office, he was a timber merchant in Mango Creek, a man of respectable business interests and apparently unblemished record. He would know who had bought the truck. But could he be relied upon to remember the name? So many soldiers passed through Mango Creek; and the local inhabitants were often prone to amnesia in their dealings with officialdom. Pollock was doubtful.

At any rate, he would try. He would go up to Mango Creek, seek out the timber merchant and discover everything he knew. If possible, he would locate the vehicle in question and impound it, pending further investigation. He would put the screws on. Someone was responsible for that signature, someone was to blame. Pollock would find out who.

Brother Micah and Brother Ton Ton lay concealed in a patch of reeds close to the river bank, their weapons trained on a lone pirogue approaching from upstream. They could make out two figures in the canoe, one in the bow and one in the stern, separated by the grey bulk of the cargo in between. The vessel was riding low in the water, propelled noiselessly by the paddles of the two Indians, their shadows vast and eerie against the rising sun. The men were alone. As agreed, they had travelled without escort and had left even their hunting weapons behind to avoid arousing suspicion.

All the same, Brother Micah was careful to scrutinise the far bank before uttering the low 'whoyou' whistle of a nightjar that was the signal for the Indians to come ashore. He scanned the foliage methodically from left to right, searching for anything out of the ordinary, a hint that the silent jungle had been disturbed in some way. He did not want any surprises. He desired no reception committee other than his own. Only when he was certain no one was watching did he rise from his hiding place and go forward with Ton Ton to meet the newcomers.

The canoe nosed into the shallows. Micah took hold of the bows while the two couriers shipped their paddles and ran the vessel into the reeds, where it could not be seen. Nobody spoke. Under Micah's direction, the Indians set to work at once to unload their cargo of tightly packed burlap bags. They worked fast, passing the bags from hand to hand and stacking them in piles on the bank. The river was regularly patrolled by a Customs launch from Mango Creek; they were anxious to get back across the border without delay.

Brother Ton Ton, meanwhile, breasted a small rise facing away from the reeds and lifted his sub-machine gun twice in the air. It was followed by the appearance of the main body of Warlocks, some eight or nine, who had been hidden in a clump of trees out of sight of the river. First to break cover was Brother Euclid, the paymaster of the movement, leading a string of donkeys roped together nose to tail. He was flanked on each side by three men armed with automatic weapons. At the rear, emerging last of all, came Leon Sullivan. He had judged it expedient to remain in the background until the contact with the Indians had been made secure.

Unsheathing his knife, Sullivan selected a number of burlap bags at random and slit them open, near the bottom. He scooped out a handful of the contents and held it up to his nose. Rolling the leaf between thumb and forefinger, he sniffed expertly. It was the real stuff all right, high grade ganja, dry, crumbly and free of seed. About a million dollars' worth, by the look of it. Sullivan exulted inwardly. Everything was going according to plan. All he had to do now was to deliver the bags to the sea, smuggle them aboard the freighter – which should be no problem – and his fortune would be made.

He put away his knife and nodded to Micah. While a lookout kept watch, the Warlocks began to load the sacks of ganja on to the backs of the uncomplaining donkeys. Each sack was secured with rope. Willing hands made short work of the task, which was carried out in silence.

When it was finished, the Indians came forward to collect their share of the takings. They had no idea of the market value of the crop. They knew it only as the Marie-Jeanne weed, which grew profusely in the jungle around their villages and could be had for the picking. The men were Tamils, simple people who measured riches in terms of rice and salt. They understood money well enough, and appreciated its use as a medium of exchange; but they had only a hazy notion of what it could buy. They were not bothered by the complexities of higher finance. As long as they had enough to purchase goats, and the occasional hunting knife, they were content.

Sullivan studied them thoughtfully. They were no longer any use to him. Indeed, as potential witnesses, they were a liability. It would be a good idea to cover his tracks. Smiling at the Indians, he drew Micah and Ton Ton aside and gave them their orders in an urgent undertone. The Warlocks grinned. They took the Indians by the elbow and escorted them down to the river where the canoe lay. All four vanished behind the reeds. A squeal, a grunt, and the tops of the reeds thrashed frantically for a few seconds. Then all was silent again – until Micah and Ton Ton came out alone and knelt down at the water's edge to clean their pangas.

'It done,' reported Micah. 'From ear to ear. We go now?'

'Yes,' said Sullivan. 'There's nothing more to do here. Tell Euclid to lead on. The transport's waiting at the village. We'll go the usual route.'

Leaving the two corpses hidden in the reeds, the party of Warlocks shouldered their weapons and set off one by one through the scrub. Brother Euclid took the bridle of the leading pack animal. Brothers Micah and Ton Ton cut themselves a switch from nearby brushwood and applied it to the donkeys' hindquarters whenever necessary. The others followed in single file, relaxed and confident, with Sullivan in his accustomed place towards the rear. They were no longer expecting trouble. If the Indians had been planning a double-cross, it would have been sprung by now.

The march continued several hours, with a halt at midday for a bowl of fish and brede leaves in the shade of a bamboo grove. The trail was a tortuous one, twisting back and forth among the hills and valleys, skirting swamps and overgrown ravines of precipitous descent. At first the terrain was steep and virgin, untouched by the hand of man. Later the slopes gave way to a flatter, broader stretch of forest, mainly teak or ebony, with here and there an open space where timber contractors from far away had stripped the land to feed the lumber mill at Mango Creek. In such an open space lay the village of Regret.

Why it was called Regret, no one had ever known. Its origins were obscure. It was a logging camp, a trading post for the woodcutters and cinnamon pickers who worked the surrounding area. Its only permanent inhabitants were six families of maroons, descendants of runaway slaves, under the nominal leadership of a toothless old sot who claimed the title of headman. He lived for the sugary brew which itinerant lumberjacks gave him in return for the use of his women. Like all the men in the village, he had adopted the wearing of European clothes. The women too were dressed in European clothes – up to the waist. Above the waist they wore nothing, but went bare-breasted. The children were all naked.

The headman smiled uncomfortably at the Warlocks' approach, exposing his purple gums. He knew enough to be afraid of Sullivan. Given the choice, he would have preferred that the Warlocks used some other village as a base for their clandestine activities. But he had not been given the choice.

A timber lorry was parked at the beginning of the rough dirt track which led through the jungle to the main highway, many miles distant. Between the logs a hidden space had been prepared for the cargo of marijuana. Forming a human chain, Sullivan's men unburdened the pack animals and began to transfer the sacks to their new hiding place. To all intents and purposes, a simple lumber wagon, decked out in a red flag, would be setting out on a normal commercial run to Mango Creek and thence to the sea. Only Leon Sullivan would know how much the cargo was really worth.

'We'll rest here for a while before we move on,' he told Micah. 'Three of us will take the truck. You, me and Ton Ton. The others can go back to camp. We shan't need them any more.'

Micah had been hoping for a halt. His eye, roving speculatively around the village, had already come to rest on the young face of one of the headman's many daughters. From behind her father's elbow she had returned his gaze. Micah burned with anticipation. Putting down his rifle, he laid out a handful of ganja taken from the burlap bags and started to roll a cigar-sized joint. He and the girl would smoke it between them. It was better to come bearing gifts; it made relations more amicable, and Micah was ever an amicable man. He liked to give pleasure. Afterwards, if she had been good, he would let her have some to keep.

Malcolm Pollock had had a frustrating day. He had been obstructed at every turn. His every inquiry about Bedford lorries had been met with blank stares and faces of squat incomprehension. Though they listened to him with polite respect, no one understood him, no one knew what he was talking about. He was not getting through.

He spent some time at the timber yard, whose owner – unearthed, reluctantly, from behind a stack of kindling – proved of little help. Yes, the owner remembered selling the lorry to the army. Yes, he remembered who had bought it. It had been a British soldier. Dressed in green, name of Pollock. The owner remembered the name quite distinctly. The world was not so well endowed with such people that he could afford to forget them. Unfortunately, however, his command of English did not enable him to enlarge on that description. The purchaser was tall and green; that was as much as he could say.

Nor did he see fit to enlarge upon the present whereabouts of the lorry in question. It lay where 9 Platoon had left it, submerged in water beside the bridge. It did not occur to the owner to pass on this information. He presumed the army knew it already. As far as he was concerned, the English would have to sort it out among themselves. If they wanted to pay him good money to take away his derelict truck and dump it in the river, he wasn't going to argue. His not to reason why. Far simpler just to say nothing.

He had other motives for feigning ignorance at this particular time. Another of his vehicles was due to pass through Mango Creek shortly, and although he had been careful not to inquire too closely, he had reason to believe that it would be carrying an illicit cargo of marijuana. Leasing trucks to outside interests was a profitable sideline for the timber merchant, but one that he preferred to know little about. He did not mention it to Pollock. Idle talk about lorries, in his view, ought to be discouraged.

Reluctantly Pollock considered his next move. He could see that there was nothing further to be gained from the timber merchant. So where did he go from here? He was still no nearer to solving the problem, no nearer to getting his man. Somebody, somewhere could shed some light – but who? Privately Pollock had his own suspicions. He suspected that Sebastian Clinch knew more than he was telling. The difficulty was how to worm it out of him.

Thinking it over, Pollock decided at length on the direct approach. That seemed the most sensible. He would go to Clinch now, he would confront him with the timberman's evidence and he would demand a confession. Gentleman to gentleman. If Pollock threatened to arrange a meeting between the two, Clinch would surely have no choice but to come clean. It would be embarrassing, most embarrassing, but Pollock could see no alternative if Clinch was to be made to do the decent thing.

Steeling himself for the encounter, Pollock put his Landrover into gear and accelerated rapidly out of the yard. He turned on to the main highway and pressed his foot down. In his head he rehearsed the scene with Sebastian, looking at it from all angles, preparing a position to cover every eventuality. Whatever else might happen, there could be no further compromise on his part. He was not going to be brushed off a second time.

The highway was almost deserted. The only other vehicle in sight was a Bedford lorry approaching at right angles from a side road. It was carrying a load of timber, to which a red warning flag had been tied. Pollock squinted obliquely at the lorry, at the name of the timber yard painted in white on the side, at the apprehensive faces of the three black men in the driving cab, and knew instinctively that something was up. A hunch, a sixth sense for wrongdoing, the same hunch that had put the wine waiter in Colchester and would shortly unmask Sebastian, told him that here was a part of the jigsaw. Pollock glinted. He was on to it at last. Glancing over his shoulder, he put out an arm and spun the wheel.

Brother Micah, who was driving, slammed his foot on the brake as the Landrover slewed across their path. Leon Sullivan and Brother Ton Ton were powerless to do anything. They could only sit and watch, helpless, as Pollock came towards them, his face set and determined, his step heavy with officialdom.

Opening the nearside door of the cab, Pollock motioned them out. He extended his hand for Micah's licence. 'Is this your vehicle?' he demanded.

'No sir.' It was Sullivan who answered. 'It's not ours. It belongs to the timber company.'

Pollock wasn't satisfied. He knew evasiveness when he saw it. He looked more closely at the speaker and recognised the man's face at once. A Warlock, wanted for some crime. Foxtrot had circulated the photo. Searching the recesses of his mind, Pollock spoke without thinking.

'You're that murderer...' he said. They were his last words.

Brother Ton Ton had been trained to kill quickly and quietly. A single slash of the knife did for Pollock. Wordlessly the body of the late lieutenant fell to earth and lay sprawled in the dust. It twitched a bit, shuddered – and became still. The Warlocks were appalled.

'*Jesus*!' said Sullivan.

'Look like de revolution begun,' said Micah.

'What we do now?' demanded Ton Ton.

Sullivan was already climbing into the cab. 'We must get out of here. Back to the jungle. They'll be looking for tyre marks. We'll have to ditch the lorry and hide up somewhere while they search for us.'

Micah slammed the door and started the motor. Dust flew as he drove the front wheels over Pollock's recumbent corpse. The lorry continued for a dozen yards, then drew up, its engine still running. Sullivan got out and doubled back to the body. He was carrying a panga.

'May as well be hanged for a sheep as a lamb,' he told himself. He swung the panga.

12

HEADLESS KILLER DRAMA.
DASHING PEER LEADS HUNT. POLICE BAFFLED
By William Hogan

A ring of steel has been thrown around the island of Casuarina following the murder yesterday of Malcolm Pollock, the British Army lieutenant whose dismembered body was discovered near Mango Creek.

In a dramatic bid to track down the killers, men of the Gobelin Guards have sealed the border with Santa Monica and are scouring the jungle near the scene of the crime.

They are led by dashing major The Earl of Malplaquet, family motto 'Summus locus omnia vincit'.

The Earl, who was educated at Millfield, said: 'I am confident I shall catch the murderers before long and bring them to justice.'

He declined to comment on reports that Pollock's head had been seized by Warlocks for use in a voodoo ceremony.

'It *was* murder, was it?' asked Malplaquet. 'I understand Pollock left rather a large mess bill. You don't suppose he could have committed suicide?'

'He would have shot himself,' said Foxtrot. 'He wouldn't have cut his head off.'

'Ah.'

'It couldn't have happened at a worse time,' Foxtrot went on. 'We're going home. I just got word this morning. We've been given a definite departure date – next month, just in time for Christmas. A battalion of Highlanders is due to relieve us. They'll laugh themselves silly if we hand over the command in the state it is now. So will the French. We're going to have to get hold of those killers before the Jocks arrive. Otherwise we'll never hear the end of it.'

Lord Malplaquet wanted no reminder of the need for success. He wasted little time. Summoning the Company clerk, he called for an O group to attend at HQ Battle Group Blenheim. The platoon commanders of 7, 8 and 9 Platoons and their respective gold-sergeants joined him in the tent.

'We're working blind at the moment,' he began. 'We don't know where to look. All we can do is send out patrols into the jungle and see what they turn up. The killers must be in there somewhere. Foxtrot says there must have been at least three, judging by the footprints. If we keep hammering at them, sooner or later something is bound to give. I've worked out a schedule for the Company. 7 and 8 Platoons will patrol the jungle; section strength, two-day efforts at first – one day out, the second back in. 9 Platoon will be on road blocks.'

Road blocks. Sebastian drew a rude picture in his notebook. Searching cars was nobody's idea of soldiering. It was a policeman's job.

'I don't expect you to find anything,' Malplaquet told him. 'The idea is to keep the killers off the roads. Once they know you're covering the area, they'll think twice about moving too far.'

'What kind of road blocks? Deliberate, or snap?'

'Snap. Word will soon get around. Run them for an hour or so, then try somewhere else. You know the form.'

Sebastian did indeed. It was standard internal security procedure. Rat traps to catch the unwary. A sudden swoop occasionally paid dividends; more often it did not.

'I'll need dannert coils,' he said. 'And knife rests.'

'It's all taken care of. The kit is outside. Foxtrot laid it on.' Malplaquet looked round the circle. 'This is more than just a police action. It's a flag-waving operation. You must show the flag, all of you, show them that they can't get away with killing a white man on the open highway. Search everything you come across – vehicles, and pedestrians too, everything. Don't stand any nonsense. Be firm. Show these people that the Queen's writ still runs, even in the jungle. Keep them on their toes. That's the way to deal with them.'

The council of war broke up. Sebastian ducked under the camouflage net and joined Sergeant Ball outside. The ground was wet underfoot. Lord Malplaquet's HQ was a stark, damp place, situated on the spur of a hill, swept continually by mist and rain. It was known to the locals as Bout-du-monde, because they had never seen anything like it on earth. It could have been Wales, rather than the Indian Ocean.

Halfway down the hill, a patch of level ground had been cleared and Dayglo panel markers laid out for helicopter landings. Two Alouette helicopters, manned by French pilots, were parked on hessian mats to prevent them sinking into the ooze. Beyond them stood a pair of three-ton lorries loaded with road-block equipment, which had arrived from Fort Pitt earlier in the day. 9 Platoon were drawn up in sections beside the trucks, wearing skeleton order, waiting for Ball and Sebastian to take delivery of the consignment.

The driver produced an inventory and asked for a signature. The list ranged in scope from tables and chairs to torches, shovels, barriers and striped wooden poles. It would all have to be identified. Motioning the platoon aboard the transport, Sergeant Ball joined Sebastian and began to check the items one by one.

The Guardsmen were in good spirits. The news of Pollock's death, and the manner of it, had made a deep impression on them. It appealed to their sense of drama. It was something to discuss, something to write home about. Partridge had been there when the police brought the body in. For the hundredth time, as the soldiers boarded the trucks, he recounted how he had seen the corpse carried on a stretcher, how the gendarmes had covered it with a groundsheet, how one dead hand had trailed down limply towards the ground. The story had grown and been embellished with each telling. It would not be long before Partridge came to believe that he himself had been a witness to the murder.

Turtle, alone, paid no attention to Partridge's tale. There was something on his mind. Instead of joining the others in the back of the truck, he stood by himself a little way off, hanging behind, speaking to no one, taking no part in the proceedings. He was preoccupied with his own thoughts, anxious to be relieved of a private burden. He was waiting for a chance to talk to Sebastian.

It was now or never. Warily, Turtle made his approach. 'I was wondering if I could have a word with you, sir,' he said.

'Probe, 3 foot, *one*. Prodder, 4 foot, *one*. Tape measure, *one*. Yes, Turtle, what is it?'

'Not here, sir. In private.' Turtle was unhappy. 'It's personal, like.'

'Fingerprint pad, *one*. Stop signs, luminous, *two*. That's the lot, Sarnt Ball. All right, Turtle, but it'll have to be quick. There's a lot to do.'

Leading Sebastian away from the others, Turtle kept his voice low. 'It's like this,' he said. 'I've been walking out with Adelita – you know her, sir, the girl in the film – and we're in love. We want to get married.'

Sebastian was incredulous. 'You can't be serious, Turtle. Good heavens, you only met the girl a couple of weeks ago. You hardly know her.'

'It's long enough. We just sort of clicked, sir, soon as we saw each other. We knew there could never be anyone else for either of us. Not ever.'

The bombshell could not have been worse timed. The men aboard the trucks were already beginning to fidget. Unwillingly, helplessly almost, Sebastian tore his thoughts away from road blocks and murder, and addressed himself to this new, unwelcome complication. He had no difficulty recognising the language of schoolgirl vapouring. Turtle, poor fool, was too young and too stupid to know his own mind. Sebastian would have to save him from himself. To be kind, he would first have to be cruel. Turtle would not thank him for it.

'She's a hooker, you know that. Two bucks a bang and no questions asked.'

'Not any more.' Turtle shook his head. 'She was only doing that until she could find a better job. Things'll be different in England.'

'A *prostitute*, Turtle! A whore! A woman who sells her body for money. Think of all the men who've been through her before you. Think, Turtle, think!'

'That's all in the past now. She'll never have to do that again. Once we're in England, in a married quarter, she'll be my wife. She'll have me to take care of her. I'll always be there to protect her. She won't have to worry about a thing.'

So that was his game. Sebastian could see it now. Turtle the waif, object of scorn and derision, had found someone in need of his protection. Someone, as he imagined, more inept than himself. That Adelita was well able to look after her own interests had probably never entered his head. He saw only a woman desperate for an aeroplane ticket and a place to go in England, both of which, as a British soldier, he was in a position to supply.

'Have you thought this thing through properly?' Sebastian asked. 'There's a waiting list for married quarters, you know. You won't get one straight away. You'll have to wait a while.'

'She can stay with my mum, sir. Up in Wolverhampton.'

'But will she be happy there?'

'We'll manage, sir. Things'll work out.'

'And what about the age difference? You're only eighteen. She must be a lot older than you.'

'Twenty-five. Only seven years.' That was a lie, for a start. Adelita was being modest. By Sebastian's reckoning she would never see thirty again.

'I think you should wait a bit,' he told Turtle. 'There's no hurry, after all. Why not carry on as you are, for the time being at least? Get to know each other better. See how it goes.' This was subterfuge. Like any fond parent, Sebastian calculated that the romance would fizzle out within a few weeks – especially if Sergeant Ball made sure that Turtle was kept busy from morning till night, with no chance to slip away and meet the object of his desire. And if, in spite of everything, he stuck to his guns, Sebastian would see to it that he was sent back to England on the next plane, safe for ever from Adelita's clutches. Lord, how Turtle would hate him.

'No sir, I'm quite sure in my own mind it's what I want to do. Adelita and me, we've talked it over, see, and we know what we're doing. It's all fixed up. I've got my pay, and she can get a job. The army'll give us a quarter. We'll live there with her little girl. We'll be all right.'

'She's got a daughter?'

'Yes sir, a little girl. I'm going to adopt her.'

What a mess! Sebastian swore. Why did Turtle have to do this to him? Of all the women in the world, why did he have to pick a harpy for his bride? With a child, as well. It was too much. To cap it all, the future well-being of all three now depended on Sebastian, who wanted nothing to do with it. Or, if not on him, on Malplaquet. Here, at least, was a way out. If he was careful, he would be able to pass on to Malplaquet the blame for Turtle's ruined happiness. Let him be the one to wear the horns.

'There isn't time to talk about it now,' he said. 'It will have to go to the Company commander. I'll speak to him later. He'll decide what's to be done. Until then, let's leave things as they are. No need to rush – if it comes off like you think it will, you'll have the rest of your lives together.'

That was the way to play it. Stall Turtle and keep him occupied until Adelita had faded from memory. It would not be long. Knowing Turtle, he would probably want to marry someone else next week. Meantime, and much more urgently, there were Pollock's killers to attend to.

About five miles from Mango Creek, the road to the sea doubled back on itself around a rocky outcrop covered with trees. Sebastian placed his road block on the S bend, where it would be invisible from both directions. Motorists with something to hide would be in the middle of the army before they had a chance to reverse.

The platoon drove to the spot in the two lorries. Guardsmen were already streaming over the tailboards as the drivers edged their vehicles off the road into the trees. Each man knew the drill. Each had his own task, to which by temperament he was best suited. Partridge's job was to flag down the traffic. Gilligan manned one of the backstops. He was to impede the progress of anybody attempting to escape on foot. Turtle did the same for motor vehicles. Armed with a length of spiked chain, he was detailed to conceal himself in the undergrowth a little way ahead of the checkpoint. If any motorist tried to flee with scorched tyres, Turtle had orders to heave the chain under its wheels and scupper the getaway vehicle. He was then to arrest the occupants at gunpoint.

Everybody was working at once. Small parties of Guardsmen doubled along the road, lugging knife rests into position and setting up red-painted Stop signs ahead of the barriers. Ball strode back and forth, encouraging some men and shouting at others, keeping a close eye on all that was going on. Sebastian walked around the perimeter and sited the backstops along likely escape routes. Gilligan installed himself in a gully leading away from the road towards the jungle. Turtle disappeared into the bushes with his length of chain. Inside five minutes, the road block was open for business.

Their first customer proved something of a disappointment. He appeared almost at once, a pedestrian, a wizened Malabar in white cotton pyjamas and bare feet, approaching from the direction of the sea. Behind him trailed an equally old mule. Thrown across the mule's withers were two large wicker panniers, one containing pineapples, the other sugar cane. It must have been market day somewhere.

Deadpan and silent, the Malabar proceeded on foot towards the platoon, little knowing that Turtle was watching his every move from the depths of the roadside. His sad old Asiatic face was deep-wrinkled with age. Down the centre of the road he came, looking neither to the left of him nor to the right. The only sound was the regular clip-clop of the mule's hooves, following patiently in his wake.

It seemed unnecessary to stop and search such a harmless old man, but Sebastian's orders had been explicit. Everyone was to be frisked, without exception. It was a propaganda exercise as much as anything. The aim was to impress upon the population that a British officer could not be murdered without the certainty of immediate retribution.

On reaching the barrier, the Malabar came to a stop. He looked round. A ring of Guardsmen stepped forward to do him over. Partridge asked him politely to raise his arms. His features remained expressionless as he did what he was told.

Partridge ran his fingers expertly over the old man's body and squeezed his clothing between finger and thumb to establish that he was carrying no concealed weapons. Armpit and crotch were the usual hiding places. The old man made no protest.

'He's clean,' Partridge reported.

'Show him the picture,' said Ball.

The picture was of Pollock as the Warlocks had left him. The old man peered blankly at it. It meant nothing to him. Nor did a second picture, a mugshot of Pollock, taken from the victim's passport.

The old man shook his head. He could shed no light on the mystery. Behind him, a bus which had crept up unobserved began to disgorge passengers at the barrier. It was the market day special, bound for Mango Creek. It was filled with men and women of every shade *en route* from the outlying villages to sell their wares in town. The passengers were accompanied by goats and chickens, which travelled with them inside the vehicle. Fruit baskets, tin trunks and untidy bales of coloured cloth were stacked on the roof, which could be reached by a ladder positioned above the near-side rear wheel. Two bicycles were tied to the back, obscuring the rear window above the spare tyre.

The occupants were crowding the aisle, impatient to join the throng at the barrier. They were intrigued by the idea of a road block. Clutching their possessions, they hastened to disembark. The leaders gathered curiously around the two photos and passed them from hand to hand.

'The old man wants to know if he can go now,' said Ball. 'He might as well, sir. There's nothing he can do to help.'

'All right. Let him go. But get him to sign a No complaints chit first.'

Soon the search teams had their hands full persuading the bus passengers to stand in an orderly queue and remain segregated until each had been frisked. At first the passengers were disposed to be cheerful. The idea of a checkpoint was a new one on them and they were willing to give it a try. But when the Guardsmen climbed on to the roof of the bus and began to open the bundles, their owners became resentful. This was an intrusion upon privacy. Although the soldiers did the work with delicacy and tact, as they had been trained to do, the travellers were not placated. Their mood changed from stoic to querulous. They began to complain.

A battered yellow hire-car pulled up behind the bus. Willie Hogan got out. He did not enter the checkpoint, but stood watching from the other side of the barrier. He was carrying a portable typewriter.

'What's going on here?' he demanded, waving an arm at the mob, who had now overwhelmed the road block. 'Who are all these people? What are you doing to them?'

'We're extending our peace-keeping role in support of the civil power,' Sebastian told him.

'Harassing the wogs?'

'Hardly.'

'The old man says he can't write,' reported Ball. 'He's illiterate.'

'It looks to me as if you're harassing them.'

'Get him to sign an X.'

'If you're not harassing them, why are they so angry?'

'He won't do it, sir. He refuses. He says he won't sign anything he can't read.'

'They're not angry. They're just a little upset, that's all. Okay then, just let him go anyway.'

'If you say so, sir.'

The search of the bus and its occupants disclosed two items of interest. A one-eyed negro, an evil-looking man, was revealed to be carrying a panga on his person. The weapon was swiftly confiscated and its owner frogmarched to the interrogation table. Further investigation proved him to be a pillar of the local community, a church-going greybeard who used the panga to cut sugar cane on his plantation. It was not his fault that he had only one eye; there was no law against looking sinister. With profuse apology, Sebastian returned the weapon to him and ordered his release.

The other item was more important. A routine search of a young black girl's hand luggage had revealed a small quantity of marijuana carried openly in a skin pouch. The girl, a maroon from the jungle, pleaded ignorance of the law. She spoke no English, but argued her case through interpreters. She did not know that ganja was illegal. The substance had been given to her by a friend. She did not know his name. He was a negro, one of a party of Warlocks, and she had met him in the back country at a place called Regret. Two days ago. She had no idea where he was now.

Sebastian was inclined to believe her. The girl looked innocent enough. Bare breasts and guile made unlikely companions. There was nothing to be gained from pressing charges – he decided instead to let her off with a warning. In sign language he delivered a stern admonition and pointed out the error of her ways. The girl heeded him dutifully, but without comprehension. She did not understand what she had done wrong. She knew only that she was being rebuked. She could not imagine why.

Chastened, she rejoined the other travellers in the bus. Sebastian watched her go. He had confiscated her marijuana. He intended to give it to the intelligence section, along with the story about Regret. It might mean something to Foxtrot; if not, the gendarmes would certainly want to know.

Sebastian called it a day soon afterwards and ordered a return to Mango Creek. The road block had lost the element of surprise. Of Pollock's murderers, whoever they might be, the platoon had seen not a whisker. They had learned nothing of significance. As an exercise in public relations, the operation had enjoyed only mixed success – had perhaps done more harm than good. All they had to show for their efforts was a pocketful of marijuana, enough for two smokes – hardly a satisfactory outcome.

Some hours later, Leon Sullivan held a meeting in the jungle to discuss 9 Platoon's activities, news of which had reached him circuitously from half a dozen sources aboard the market bus.

'They're covering the roads,' he told the others. 'It's still too dangerous to travel. We can't move by lorry. We shall have to keep lying low for a day or two, until we find out which way the wind is blowing.'

'And the ganja?' asked Brother Euclid. 'It is safe?'

'It's safe. Micah and Ton Ton have seen to that. They've hidden it where no one will find it unless they know what they're looking for. Certainly not a British soldier. And if anyone does come across it, they'll be in for a shock. We've left something behind for them to remember us by. Something they won't forget in a hurry.'

On the way back to Mango Creek, Sebastian made a short detour to call in at Mme Boongay's. He wanted to see Adelita. He did not expect to get any sense out of her, but he owed it to Turtle to try.

His conversations with Adelita had always been monosyllabic, and this one was no exception. The situation was not improved by Mme Boongay, who established herself on a chair between them and undertook to conduct negotiations on behalf of her client. To Mme Boongay, a practical woman, this proposed marriage was a godsend. The holy state of matrimony, *per se*, had nothing to do with it. Great Britain – land of milk and honey, of Royal Family and national health – was the prize. Mme Boongay's sitting-room was plastered with magazine cuttings of the Queen and her children. By marrying Turtle, Adelita would be entering a new and alluring world. Mme Boongay was all for it.

'But does she really love him?' asked Sebastian. 'That's the point. It would be futile to get married just so she can live in England. She'd hate it.'

'*Course* she loves him. Adelita a clever girl. She know what she doin', no mistake about dat.'

Sebastian looked at Adelita. 'Is that true? Do you really want to marry Turtle? Or are you only using him to get an entry permit to England?'

Adelita made no reply. She simply stared insolently. She tilted her chin and defied Sebastian to break her hold on Turtle. Adelita didn't love him. She knew it, and Sebastian knew it, and there wasn't a blind thing he could do to let Turtle in on the secret. Adelita had got him where she wanted him. Silly bitch.

13

What about this man Sullivan, whose face seemed so familiar? Why couldn't Sebastian place him? He had a good memory for faces, or so he thought, but this one escaped him. Yet he was certain he had seen Sullivan before. Not as a Warlock, because that would have made a lasting impression on him. Perhaps as an ordinary negro, encountered somewhere on the platoon's travels around the island. But where?

He took his worries to Foxtrot, who had set up shop at Battle Group Blenheim.

'Tell me again what you know about him,' said Sebastian. 'Maybe there's something in his background that'll give me a clue.'

'There's not much to tell. His background is uncertain. The gendarmes don't seem to know anything – at least, I haven't been able to get any sense out of them. He's in his late twenties. He's got a sharp brain, and he's had military training from somewhere. There's no doubt on that score. Other than that, I know nothing.'

'You must know something.'

'I told you. Nothing.'

Foxtrot was in a bad humour, and with good reason. The mail had just come in by helicopter from Fort Pitt. There had been a postcard for Captain Duff-Barrington-Gore from the Oxford and Cambridge Examinations Board: '*I am sorry to say that you were not successful in the recent A Level History examination.*' To his chagrin, Foxtrot's hopes of quitting the army and becoming a barrister had been destroyed. His future had foreclosed on him. He was doomed to follow the drum.

The blow had come at a particularly unfortunate time, for he was embroiled with Lord Malplaquet in a dispute over tactics, and could have done with some cheer to lighten his load. The dispute concerned Regret, the trading post alleged to be the source of the marijuana discovered by 9 Platoon. For want of any more promising lead, Foxtrot was in favour of sending a recce patrol to Regret, in conjunction with air support, to stake out the surrounding terrain. If Pollock's murder could be linked to that of the woman found floating in Mango Creek, both of them mutilated in the style of Leon Sullivan, then it followed that the presence of an armed band of Warlocks at Regret might lead to the unravelling of the mystery. It was certainly worth investigating. Foxtrot had said as much to Malplaquet. He had also drawn up a plan. And that had been his undoing.

Malplaquet refused to take action. He was not going to be stampeded by subordinates. He suspected Foxtrot of attempting to force the issue, of seeking the initiative for a triumph that should rightly belong to him. If any capital was going to be made out of Pollock's murder, Malplaquet would not be sharing it with junior officers. Rather than do what Foxtrot suggested, he would, if pushed, send out patrols in the opposite direction.

Foxtrot had pleaded with him, arguing the need for swift action if the Warlock suspects were to be picked up, but Malplaquet stood firm. There was more involved here than a simple disagreement over tactics. Military discipline was at stake. He could not be seen to be influenced from below, especially not with the promotion board watching over him. He would make his own decisions, in his own good time, and nothing Foxtrot could do or say – no matter how pertinent – would have the slightest effect. Malplaquet was not going to be moved. He had dug his heels in.

It was in this uncompromising mood that Sebastian found Malplaquet when he dropped in to the HQ tent to make a formal application of marriage on behalf of Turtle. Sebastian was not anticipating any support on the issue from the Company Commander, and he found none. Malplaquet wouldn't listen to a word.

'Don't bother me with that. I haven't time to concern myself with Turtle's personal affairs. It's your problem. Tell him he can't get married and that's the end of it.'

'He's submitted his request in writing. There are no legitimate grounds for refusing it.'

'You can find a way.'

'Not legally, I can't.'

'I just don't want to know. Do whatever you like. Lock him up, if you have to. Only don't get me involved.'

But Turtle had already taken matters into his own hands. Love, and the urgency of youth, had made him desperate. Abandoning his customary diffidence, he came to Sebastian in a mood verging almost on the truculent.

'Sir, I'd like to have this afternoon off,' he said. 'Just a couple of hours. So's I can get married. My girl's got a priest fixed up in Mango Creek. Two hours, sir, that's all we need.'

'Turtle, it's out of the question! You can't go and charge into marriage, not just like that.' Sebastian groped for words. How could he explain? 'It's your whole life. It's not something to be casual about. I can't allow you to do it. I won't.'

'*Please*, sir. They're expecting me. I gave my word. It's hearts and minds, sir, that's what it is. If I don't turn up, they'll think I was bluffing my way. Straight up.'

'No, Turtle. I'm sorry. This is for your own good. Marry in haste, repent at leisure. Surely you know that?'

Turtle was respectful. 'I don't want to cause no trouble, sir, but I know my rights. If I want to get married, you're not allowed to stop me. It's a free country. I can do what I like.'

'Maybe so. But not in army time. You asked for leave, and you're not going to get it. I'm afraid the army can't spare you this afternoon.'

'Why not? What are we doing that's so important?'

'Turtle, I'm not going to argue with you. I have said that you can't have leave. That's all there is to it. Now go away.'

Against his own inclination, Malplaquet had been forced to conclude that there might be something in this business of Regret. It was, as Foxtrot said, too important to ignore. Questions might be asked, inquiries made, if he did nothing. So, after a suitable lapse of time to establish his independence, he held a Company O group to which all officers except Foxtrot were invited.

'I'm going to send out a platoon,' he announced. '7 Platoon. I've given a warning order to the quartermaster-sergeant. He's working on it now. Timings are as follows: collect stores immediately after this briefing, reveille 0400 tomorrow morning, move out at first light.'

'How long will we be gone?' asked 7 Platoon's commander.

'Four days should do it. A day to get there, two days checking out the location, a day to get back. Longer, if you need it. I'm asking the French for helicopter time. Provided the weather stays fine, you can be resupplied from the air.'

'Action on meeting suspects?'

'Pull them in. They're probably carrying small arms, but don't shoot unless they shoot first. Don't let them get away either. They're needed alive for questioning.'

'What about friendly forces? Are there any other troops in the area?'

'None. You'll be on your own. Keep in radio contact as long as you can – your call-sign is 31 Tango. Once out of range, you'll have to rely on your air support for communication. The chopper will be out looking for you at dawn on Day Two. Use it as an extra pair of eyes. The killers must have a camp somewhere. If they've camouflaged it at ground level, they may have forgotten to disguise it from the air.'

31 Tango scribbled busily. He was a correct young man, newly commissioned from Sandhurst, who had joined the battalion with the last draft from England. His face still carried the pimples of adolescence. Less than a year ago he had been a schoolboy.

Malplaquet pushed a folder towards Sebastian. It contained aerial photographs of the Regret region. They had originally been addressed to Foxtrot, but had been intercepted in the mail by Malplaquet. 'You're to work with 31 Tango as air liaison rep,' he told Sebastian. 'You'll fly in the helicopter and keep an eye out for suspects. Call-sign Kestrel. If you see anything interesting, get in touch with the ground forces and have them look into it. Tents, thatched huts, camp fires – anything that looks unusual. Anything out of the ordinary.'

That was something, at any rate. Sebastian disliked flying, but found it preferable to road control. He examined the photographs. Under a stereoscope, the terrain revealed a mixture of swamp and steep hills, covered in forest. Rough country. It would be hard going for 31 Tango and his men. Not for Sebastian, though. He would be skimming the tree-tops, seeking out targets and guiding the infantry on to them from overhead – skilled work, but relatively painless.

In the Warlock camp, time was running short. Leon Sullivan weighed up the information brought in by his scouts and balanced it against further considerations known only to himself. The problem was the ganja crop. According to schedule, the American freighter was due to dock shortly at Englishtown. It would not spend long in harbour. There was little margin for error if the ganja was to be smuggled aboard. The Warlocks would have to move soon, or not at all.

Sullivan pondered his options. The scouts had reported a slackening of military interest in road blocks. Transport appeared to be moving freely again along the highways. And although troop movements had been observed inside the jungle, the patrols had been few and far between. They posed little direct threat to the Warlocks. Sullivan had great faith in the junglecraft and military efficiency of his own men. He took a pride in their performance. He had trained them himself.

The British could be handled. Sullivan was certain of that. Even with increased military surveillance, a small escort of Warlocks could easily slip through the jungle unnoticed. They had done it often enough before. He would have preferred to wait a while longer, to give the air a chance to clear, but time was not on his side. There was a fortune waiting for him on that freighter. It was worth the risk.

Sullivan made his decision. He called for Micah. The operation would go ahead as planned.

'Any truth to the rumour that you've forbidden Turtle to attend his own wedding?' asked Willie Hogan, who had the newspaperman's knack of always putting in an appearance where he was not wanted.

'Some,' agreed Sebastian. He was deep in maps and photographs, attempting to familiarise himself with the landscape around Regret.

'Turtle's too young to know what's good for him. I'm not letting him rush into something he'll regret later.'

'Is that fair? It's his life, not yours.'

'Of course it's fair. Turtle would be throwing himself away on that girl. I won't let him do it.'

'What's wrong with her?'

Sebastian put down the map. 'Obviously the girl is unsuitable. Of low moral character. She's not good enough for him.'

'Un-suitable ... low moral character,' wrote Hogan.

'All this is off the record, of course.'

'No it isn't. You should have said so up front if it wasn't for publication.' He closed his notebook with a snap. *'Love's labours lost as Army says No.* It'll make an excellent headline.'

'You're not really going to quote me?'

'Yes I am.'

That did it. Cornered, Sebastian lowered his flag without a fight. 'All right,' he said. 'All right. Okay. If Turtle wants to marry her, then let him. It's his funeral. I wash my hands of the whole affair.'

Sebastian was angry with himself. He had been outmanoeuvred. Somehow events had slipped out of his control. Though he admitted no responsibility for what was happening, he had an uneasy suspicion deep down that he had not handled it well.

Turtle's face glowed with the news. 'You won't be sorry, sir. We've got a good thing going, Adelita and me. It'll work out fine, I promise.'

'We'll see. Where is the wedding?'

'In Mango Creek. The church in Regent Street. You *are* going to come, sir, aren't you? It's my big day. I'd like you to be there.'

At least Sebastian could capitulate with grace. 'Of course I'll be there,' he said. It would have been unforgivable to refuse the invitation. 'And while we're at it, I suppose you'd better have 48 hours' leave after the ceremony. Two nights. Gives you time for a honeymoon.'

'You're a sport,' said Turtle. 'Best officer I ever served under.'

The church turned out to be a simple wooden hut with a tin roof and a crucifix at one end. It was easily recognisable from a distance by the sound of piano music emanating from the open space underneath the rafters. It was entered by a pair of double doors opening directly on to the street. Outside, a diverse collection of urchins had assembled in the dirt to admire the spectacle, for a wedding in Mango Creek was a rare event and not to be missed.

H-hour was scheduled for 1400 hrs., two o'clock in the afternoon. Turtle had instructed Sebastian to RV with him outside the building at 1350 hrs. He was already there when Sebastian arrived, wearing a new white shirt and shifting from foot to foot like a man beginning to realise the enormity of the folly he was about to commit. His moustache had come on considerably since its inception. It had assumed respectable proportions. He had even made an attempt at waxing the ends, in imitation of the Quartermaster. His hair had been brushed and his shoes polished. The lamb was ready for slaughter.

Among the white men grouped together in the sunlight, an air of nervousness prevailed. Turtle was decidedly ill at ease, expelling smoke from his nostrils and refuelling from a cigarette hidden behind his back. Sebastian was unhappy too. So was Partridge, doing the honours as best man. Only Hogan, matchmaker extraordinary, seemed unaffected. He said nothing, but surveyed the others with the detached gloom of a journalist deprived of a good story.

At five minutes to two, Turtle spun his last cigarette into the dust – where it was fought over half-heartedly by the attendant children – and slunk into church. He and Partridge took their places at the front, opposite the pastor, a grizzled old negro with ash-grey hair who scrutinised them over the top of his hymn book. The pastor's wife played Creole tunes on the piano to entertain a swaying, hand-clapping congregation which had settled in for a good time and did not mean to be disappointed. The church was full. It was evident that Adelita had a large following. Sebastian had no idea she was so popular.

At half past two, thirty minutes behind schedule, the bride arrived. She made no apology for being late. As an army wife, she still had much to learn. She bounced in as if nothing was wrong, clad, Sebastian was interested to see, all in white. She was wearing a tightly cut dress that reached down to the floor, high-heeled slippers, and a veil covering her face. Her hands were folded around a bouquet of red, pink and yellow hibiscus flowers. Credit where it was due, she looked a treat. Sebastian wouldn't have minded a crack at her himself.

'Here come de bride, here *come* de bride!' sang the congregation as Adelita advanced down the aisle to take station alongside Turtle. Her train was shared between her daughter – a tiny coffee-coloured child of about four – and Mme Boongay's cherry girl, now fully gone in pregnancy. The bridesmaids were dressed in shocking pink. There were three of them, A and B Pack and Whiplash Wilma, all in a state of emotion. Tears were visible too in the eyes of Mme Boongay and Mrs Dogend, matrons of honour. They viewed the occasion as one for weeping.

Although he was called as a witness to sign the register, Sebastian remembered little of the actual ceremony. It followed the usual course. 'Do you Paul, take Adelita....?' inquired the priest, and Turtle said he did. A ring, bought from an Indian trader for several times its value, was produced from Partridge's pocket and placed on Adelita's finger. The pastor pronounced them man and wife, whereupon Mrs Adelita Turtle became a citizen of Great Britain, entitled to free medical care, social security and a cash bonus on any child she might subsequently produce. Then the congregation sang 'All things bright and beautiful'.

Afterwards, a reception was held at the beauty parlour. Mme Boongay declared open house. A hundred people must have crowded into the saloon, overflowing upstairs, on to the balconies and into the back yard beside the anti-tank pit. Once deep and broad, the pit was now full of rubbish, as were most of the others Sebastian had positioned around the town. A bed of glowing charcoal had been laid on top of the refuse and pieces of roasting goat flesh could be discerned among the embers. Black lentils and strange roots, coated in flies, were stacked up on coloured Tupperware dishes. There was rum and beer and Coca Cola by the crate. Also a noxious homemade brew, red in colour, which Sebastian forbade the troops to touch.

Mme Boongay had hired the Mango Creek Camtolee Band for the occasion, an eight-man combo of iridescent musicians led by a flame-shirted acrobat whose sleeves reached down to his ankles. Rolling his eyeballs, he dedicated his music to Turtle, the radiant bridegroom:

Will his love be like his rum?

Yes it will, yes it will.

Intoxicatin' all night long?

Yes it will, yes it will.

Everybody

Drink, drink dis toast

Drink dis weddin' toast

Drink, oh drink dis toast

To de two we love de most.

Much hand clapping and stomping of feet. Blushing, Turtle put an arm around his bride. With his free hand he raised a can of beer to her lips. Mr and Mrs Turtle! His mother would be pleased. According to the groom, the wedding was going to be announced in Wolverhampton's local paper 'just so's it's done proper'. His military training had made Turtle a stickler for the proprieties.

Everyone was dancing now, everyone except Sebastian. The wooden floor trembled to the step of Mme Boongay, an avid churchgoer, tripping out with the pastor. Partridge was renewing his acquaintance with A and B Pack. Hogan soaked quietly in a corner. 'C'mon an' dance de moutia,' crooned the singer. 'Everyone do de moutia. Père, mère, baba! Hit me now!

Jack an' Jill went up de hill

To get a little hanky panky.

Jack came back with a dollar bill

Jill came back with a Yankee!'

Sebastian stood beside the drink table, wondering how soon he could decently slip away. Seeing him alone, Mme Boongay broke loose from the preacher and took him by the arm. Her eyes were still wet and moist. She was enjoying herself hugely.

'Dis a great day for us,' she confided. 'A great day. An' a sad day, too. Never thought I goin' to lose Adelita. Never thought I see de time come.' The sentimental old harridan dabbed her eyes. 'She go far away. To England, long ways from here. But she goin' to write, tell us when she found a house. An' next year, when she settled, she send for us. We all comin' to live in London, all meet again. Some time.'

It was the drink talking – or so Sebastian hoped. He could not visualise Mme Boongay on the streets of Chelsea, a regimental camp follower. The idea was too absurd.

For a moment Mme Boongay was lost in melancholy. Then her natural courtesy reasserted itself. This was party time. 'You like a rub-out?' she inquired. 'Marche-marche? Any girl you want. You pick one, I fix. Cost nothin' today. It on de house.'

'Not for me, thank you. Some other time perhaps.'

'Sure?'

'Sure.'

'Okay, but any time you want, you just got to ask. I arrange.' She gave Sebastian a playful pinch on the nipple and moved off to speak to the band.

Sebastian left soon afterwards. He had done his duty as a guest. He shook hands with Turtle, took care not to kiss Adelita, and wished both of them good luck. Partridge was leaving too. Sebastian turned to look for him. But Turtle hadn't finished – there was something he wanted to say.

'You will send for me, sir, if there's any action? I don't want to miss nothing. I'll be here, stopping at the parlour. You won't forget, will you? I'd be pissed off if there was something going on and I wasn't around.'

'I'll see,' said Sebastian. His mind was on other matters. He had lost sight of the best man. 'Where's Partridge got to?'

He was nowhere to be found. Inquiries at the edge of the dance floor revealed that he had been seen going upstairs. The second door on the left. Sebastian put his ear against it. A string of oaths, hoarse and Anglo-Saxon, came from within. Partridge was inside, all right. And not alone.

Sebastian pushed the door open. 'Partridge, are you in there?' he demanded.

Partridge's reply was muffled, but desperate. 'Just coming, sir,' he reported.

He wasn't kidding.

14

An hour before dawn on Day Two of Operation Grass Roots (as 31 Tango's ganja-busting operation was called), Sebastian ate an early breakfast by the light of a Tilley lamp and set off to join his helicopter pilot at Battle Group Blenheim. The pilot was waiting at the landing site. He was a French marine officer in kepi and dark glasses, interested in making the acquaintance of the English. He bristled with energy and good cheer. A map of the Regret area was strapped to his left knee, and certain key features had been ringed on it in red chinagraph.

'*Bonjour*,' he said. He gripped Sebastian's hand. 'I am happy to meet you. I have been once in Ramsgate.'

They put their heads together and consulted the map. The features on the pilot's knee were also marked on Sebastian's aerial photos. Once the two were matched with the terrain on the ground, they would know where they were.

The helicopter was an Alouette – two seats in a plastic bubble, and a chain saw to hold it all together. Sebastian locked himself into the starboard side. A mouthpiece attached to his helmet kept him in touch with the pilot and also, on a different frequency, with 31 Tango's ground forces. As a precaution he was carrying a sub-machine gun and four magazines of ammunition, strapped back to back in pairs. Otherwise the helicopter was unarmed.

The pilot waited for full daylight before starting the motor. He let it run for a few moments, then gently eased the chopper into the sky, swinging the nose around until it faced the north-east. Battle Group Blenheim quickly receded from view. Before long they were over the jungle, on course for Regret. 7 Platoon had set up a forward base in the village the previous afternoon. Inquiries by 31 Tango had confirmed that a large party of Warlocks, carrying firearms, had recently passed through the area. Their present whereabouts was unknown. With help from the air, however, 31 Tango was confident of finding them within forty-eight hours.

Fifteen minutes of flying time brought the helicopter to a high range of wooded hills, beyond which lay a collection of thatched huts in an open clearing, the settlement of Regret. There could not have been more than five or six roofs visible from above. The place scarcely deserved the dignity of a name, let alone the status of village.

'Hallo Kestrel, hallo Kestrel, this is 31 Tango,' crackled the radio. 'I see you. Am displaying LP now. Over.'

'Kestrel. Roger. Out.'

Down below, a tiny green figure emerged from between the huts and inflated a yellow balloon to indicate the area prepared for landing. At the upwind edge of the clearing, a group of fluorescent panels, weighted with stones, had been laid out in the form of an H to provide a makeshift horizon. The pilot turned a gradual circle and flew into the wind, down and down, centring on the H until it was sitting just above the instrument panel. Then, with a final plop, he lowered the machine to the ground and shut off the engine. The landing was complete.

31 Tango was waiting for them. So too were the inhabitants of the village, all six families of maroons, who had plainly never before set eyes on a helicopter. Sebastian had seen them scuttle for the security of their huts as the machine landed. After a short interval, however, during which they had peeped irresolutely from behind the thatch, the villagers were persuaded to emerge and gather round this invader from the skies. Though not completely cut off from civilisation, they were far from being sophisticated. They were illiterate. They had never seen a magazine or a television or a cinema screen. They knew nothing of helicopters. Small wonder that its arrival in their midst had created a sensation.

The village headman was filled with respect. He believed that the helicopter had come from Great Britain. He suspected Great Britain of being the purple splash of land he could see in the distance. On Warlocks, he was a mine of intelligence. 31 Tango had given him to understand that information about Warlocks would be rewarded with a bottle of rum. The headman had seen many Warlocks – including Leon Sullivan, whose picture he had been shown. North, south, east and west, all directions. Several days ago. He could not say where they were now.

'I've got my point section advancing to contact,' 31 Tango told Sebastian. 'Also an OP by the edge of the swamp. They've drawn a blank so far. I'd like you to go upstairs and recce the FEBA. I thought you might catch the enemy Sunray unawares.' New to military life, 31 Tango had adopted the language of soldiering with self-conscious enthusiasm. Everything was Roger and Wilco with him. Nor did he make any secret of his pleasure at Sebastian's arrival. Since Sebastian was senior in the Army List, his presence meant 31 Tango's absolution from blame in the event of disaster.

The helicopter stayed some time on the ground while 31 Tango and the pilot worked out a flight plan to quarter the area ahead of the searching troops. The pilot elected to fly along the grid lines of the map, south to north at first, then east to west. He would search one side of the jungle, Sebastian the other. If they spotted anything, they would pass the information to the ground forces, who would carry out the leg work.

Once airborne, they made radio contact almost immediately with 31 Tango's outlying patrol. Shortly afterwards, they also had visual contact. The men were struggling up a steep slope. They looked up as the chopper flew overhead, but did not wave. Through binoculars Sebastian could imagine their lips moving as they cursed all helicopters, much as their plodding ancestors had once cursed the cavalry at Waterloo.

The patrol commander had nothing to report. In brief, staccato phrases – wasting no words – he radioed that there had been no sign of Sullivan or any of the Warlocks, nor even of ganja, which was reputed to grow wild in the forest. The only sign of life had been two itinerant calou tappers, who spoke little English and knew nothing. The patrol commander, a lance sergeant, sounded recalcitrant and sulky, as if the charms of jungle hill-climbing were wearing thin on him.

From above, too, the jungle looked empty. If there were Warlocks down below, they were keeping themselves out of sight. According to plan, the pilot criss-crossed the area from the hills on one side to the swamp on the other, but with no success. Box after box on the map revealed nothing but greenery, without even a road or river to alleviate the tedium.

Towards midday the sky began to cloud over in the east, where the regular afternoon thunderstorm was taking shape. The fuel gauge was running low. There would be time for one more sweep and then the pilot would head for home. He did not intend to be caught in the rain. Using the call-sign Kestrel, he transmitted his decision to 31 Tango. Both parties expressed regret at nothing achieved. Then the pilot set a course that would take the helicopter in a gradual curve over the jungle and across the swamp to Battle Group Blenheim.

The swamp was difficult to identify from the air. Unmarked on the map, it was overgrown with vegetation and a surface coating of weed indistinguishable from grass. In parts it was not more than six inches deep. Elsewhere, it could only be crossed by boat. Ripples of wind, shivering the muddy reflections on the surface, were often the only hint of water. A chain of islands, studded with mangrove trees, provided a home of sorts for egrets and herons. There may perhaps have been a few crocodiles in there as well. Under less demanding circumstances the swamp might have been a paradise for nature-lovers. But from where Sebastian was sitting – just above it, with the door open – the most remarkable feature about the swamp was its smell. The stink of rotting vegetation, of decay and squalor, was paramount.

Pursued by its shadow, the helicopter catapulted across the surface towards a belt of tall trees marking firmer ground the other side of the marsh. Sebastian calculated the distance at about a mile and a half. Behind them, the storm was building into a grey-black morass that threatened to obliterate the sun. Ahead, the trees came bowling forward, larger and larger, until at length they flashed underneath the chopper's belly, revealing a narrow isthmus of solid ground and a small thatched hut, almost hidden by a clump of mangrove trees leading down to the water's edge.

Sebastian got only a brief glimpse of the hut. The pilot had seen it too. He banked the chopper and curled round for another look. The building seemed in good repair, but there was no sign of life. No animals were tethered in the yard, no boat was tied to the shore, no one came out to wave. If anyone was living down there, he had little interest in helicopters.

The pilot glanced at Sebastian, then pointed downwards with his finger. He was going to land. The building might yield some information – an aged woodcutter perhaps, or a hermit who had seen the Warlocks pass this way. It was a long shot, but they had nothing better to go on.

The open space beside the hut was about twenty yards in diameter, barely adequate for a helicopter landing. The pilot was confident. He eased his machine downwards over the trees, juggled the controls, dropped first on one skid, then on the other, then both together. The rotor began to relax. The helicopter wheezed consumptively, coughed and settled down on to its haunches.

At ground level the hut was surrounded on all sides by thick scrub. It was about ten yards by five, made of bamboo poles penetrated by chinks of light. The door was simply an old piece of sacking hung across the opening. There was no one around. Feeling slightly foolish, Sebastian loaded and cocked his SMG and pointed it at the door. He knocked on the sacking. Receiving no answer, he took hold of the cloth and tore it aside – to reveal the hideous shrunken face of Malcolm Pollock mounted on a wooden pole, blocking the entrance.

The two men fell back and stared. The head was no larger than a man's fist. Its eyes were tight shut, its lips sealed with twine. It looked absurd without its spectacles.

Sebastian recovered first. Gripping his weapon, he pushed past the pilot and edged cautiously round the thing on the pole. The building was deserted. It had evidently not been used for some time. It must have been a dwelling once, because there was an open fireplace in one corner and a low-framed bed on which lay the spongy remains of a sheet made from the cork of a moho tree. About one half of the room was taken up with a pile of sacks reaching to the roof and containing the stalks of maize cobs. Underneath the maize cobs lay a million dollars' worth of marijuana.

It was still compressed into burlap bags, the way Micah and Ton Ton had left it. They had been careless. The covering of mealies was not as deep as it could have been. Sebastian did not have to look far to discover what was hidden below.

He was in a panic to get away. He had seen what lay in store if he was still around when the Warlocks came back to collect their crop. It would not do to get between a gang of armed men and a fortune, in the middle of nowhere. If there were any Warlocks in the vicinity, they could hardly have failed to notice the chopper touching down. They would already be speeding towards the hut, looking to protect their investment. It was time to go.

The pilot was of the same mind. Pausing just long enough to snatch up a fistful of ganja as evidence, he led the way back to the machine. Pollock's head was left where it was. They had seen all they needed to. The next step was to get the information back to Battle Group Blenheim, properly map-referenced, where Foxtrot could deal with it.

Twenty minutes and a fuel gauge flickering around zero brought them to the familiar green saddle of Lord Malplaquet's headquarters, a beacon of solidarity above terrain that was no longer hospitable. Sebastian had never thought he would be happy to see it. He took comfort from the vision of military activity spread out in front of him, the lines of men at the field kitchen, the ordered rows of tents, the strength and protection of a stronghold. Primitive, but reassuring. In the jungle there was danger, but not at Battle Group Blenheim. Scarcely bothering to breast the top of the hill, the pilot this time executed a perfect landing, his third of the day, and switched off the motor for good. Sebastian climbed out on legs that were slightly unsteady, nursing the enormity of their discovery. Never had he been so glad to get his feet back on the ground.

Half an hour later, Malplaquet, Foxtrot and Sebastian held a council of war in Malplaquet's tent. For once, they were all agreed on what action to take. An ambush would have to be set up on the hut, until the Warlocks came to retrieve their ganja. But what kind of ambush?

'31 Tango can't do it,' Sebastian argued. 'He'd never find his way across the swamp. It's a very difficult bit of map reading. It can only be done by someone who's already recced the area.' What was he saying? There was no one else but him. 'And it will have to be done right away. The Warlocks might go back and pick up the stuff any time. In fact they're bound to, if they saw the chopper.'

'True,' said Malplaquet. He was being strangely co-operative. 'How soon can your platoon be ready?'

Consulting his watch, Sebastian made a swift time appreciation. 'I could have them in the area by last light this evening. With an airlift, that is. Set up the ambush at once, operative first thing tomorrow morning.'

Malplaquet nodded. 'That's fine. We'll do it. Draw up a set of ambush orders and brief the Guardsmen as soon as you're ready. Hold a rehearsal, if you've got time. Give the men a chance to digest it and work out the snags. And count me in. I shall come too.'

Sergeant Ball was present at the meeting. For a moment his eyes met Sebastian's over the top of his notebook. Then, saying nothing, Ball dropped his gaze and returned to his writing.

'You're coming on the ambush?' Sebastian asked.

'I'll be supernumerary,' said Malplaquet. 'I'll be there to keep an eye on things. The operation needs two officers. It's too important to allow a cock-up.'

'But you'll be in command?'

'Not necessarily. This is a platoon performance. You will be in charge. As Company Commander, I shall stay in the background unless you need me to take over.'

Sebastian could see what was going on here. He knew Malplaquet's game. Malplaquet scented a chance to distinguish himself. It would be his command, all right, if the outcome was a success. If it failed, though, Sebastian would be the one putting on his best uniform to explain himself to the Commanding Officer.

He opened his mouth to speak, then thought better of it. There was no point arguing with Malplaquet. The ambush was the main thing. Rather than waste valuable time, he would do better to put Malplaquet out of his mind and concentrate on the operation in hand. His first responsibility was to conceive and execute a viable plan. He would do it on his own authority. If, when the time came, Malplaquet chose to interfere, there would be trouble. Sebastian would not stand for any nonsense. If necessary he would tell Malplaquet to go to hell and take command himself. But he would not cross that bridge until he came to it.

The incident rankled. Sebastian was angry with Malplaquet. As soon as the meeting broke up, he took Foxtrot aside and asked for a second opinion on how to deal with the uninvited passenger. Foxtrot's advice, though firm, was impractical.

'Shoot him if he gets out of hand,' Foxtrot said.

At 1500 hours that afternoon Sebastian held an O group for the platoon and gave them the plan. The operation was straightforward. They would be dropped in the jungle by helicopter, some distance from the target area, so as not to arouse suspicion. They would make the approach march on foot. Once in position, they would mount an ambush round the clock, day and night, for ten days, the maximum possible without resupply. If and when the Warlocks put in an appearance, the platoon would arrest them.

Using a ration carton and a groundsheet, Sebastian had assembled a makeshift model of the area around the hut as he remembered it. Two camouflage scarves indicated foliage at the edge of the swamp. Sebastian rehearsed the men thoroughly in every phase of the ambush. Every Guardsman was allotted a role and questioned closely on it. Sebastian repeated again and again the signal for opening fire –

if necessary – the signal to cease fire, what to do if the suspects appeared unexpectedly, what methods of communication to use, how to search the dead, if any. When he had finished he made the men recite it all back to him, parrot-fashion, until he was satisfied that they would know how to react in any given situation.

The men had already checked and test-fired their weapons. Rifles had been zeroed on an impromptu firing range set up in a gully. Sebastian had decided to take three machine guns. Everyone else was to carry a rifle, except the radio operator. He would be armed with a lightweight SMG.

Sergeant Ball distributed extra equipment among the Guardsmen. The load was substantial. They had to carry enough belt ammunition for the machine guns, plus rations for ten days, medical equipment, spare radio batteries and marker flares. Also a bunch of Schermuly rockets in case of emergency. Though essential, this extra weight was also a liability. If the Warlocks caught them on the march, staggering under the burden, the platoon would be in trouble.

As soon as the additional stores had been given out, Sebastian checked the men's equipment. He made each man jump up and down to see if his kit rattled, and satisfied himself that even the three identity discs around the neck were tied together with black masking tape. Shirt sleeves were rolled down and buttoned at the wrist. Hands and faces would be streaked with camouflage cream. All shiny surfaces were dulled or blackened. Nothing was left to chance.

Taking off his hat, Sergeant Ball passed it around the troops and made a collection of cigarettes, sweets and chewing gum, none of which could be taken on the ambush. The smell of tobacco was distinctive, alien to the jungle. So were sugary things and hair oil. The odour would be picked up at once by the Warlocks. From now on nobody would even wash, for fear of contaminating natural body scents with the reek of soap.

Finally, once the kit check was complete, Sebastian sent the platoon down the hill to sit on their own in the gully where the test-firing had been carried out, some distance from the rest of the camp. He wanted to isolate the patrol from those staying behind. He wanted them working and thinking together, as part of a team. There they would stay, face to face with each other, until the transport arrived.

'Take me with you, sir,' begged Turtle, who had returned from Mango Creek. 'You've got to take me. I'm here. You can't go without me.'

'What about your wife? Your new bride. What's she going to say?'

'She'll understand. We've got all the future together. She won't mind. Honest.'

'It seems a bit rough.'

Turtle was scornful. 'Nooo! My leave was up anyway. I got to do the job. It's my last chance, before the battalion goes home. A bit of action, sir, that's all I'm asking for.'

Sebastian wavered. He was reluctant to take Turtle, because if any of his men was likely to trip over his own feet and poop off an accidental gunshot in the middle of the night, Turtle was. On the other hand, Turtle was also a fully trained soldier and could not legitimately be denied a chance to ply his trade. A baptism of fire would do him good.

'All right,' he conceded. 'Go and report to Sarnt Ball. He can use an extra pair of hands. Then join the others. Fast.'

Turtle was grateful. 'Ta, sir,' he said. He was already moving off.

'Oh, and Turtle...' Sebastian called after him.

He looked back. 'Sir?'

'How was your honeymoon?'

Grinning, Turtle made an unmistakable gesture with his fist. 'Fantastic, sir. Couldn't have been better. Know what I mean?'

Right on time, two Wessex helicopters came to ferry the platoon into the jungle. They were piloted by RAF officers, the same men who irritated the Adjutant at Fort Pitt.

'I'll drop you about five thousand yards east of the ambush area,' said the pilot of the lead chopper. 'It's pretty hairy country. I'm not going to land. I'll hover for twenty seconds – not more – so your people will have to move fast and get their fingers out. If there *are* any cowboys around, my chopper will be an easy target. I won't hang about.'

Divided into two sticks, the Guardsmen were waiting in front of the helicopters at an angle of two o'clock to the cockpit. Sebastian was to fly in the first machine, Lord Malplaquet and Sergeant Ball in the second. Malplaquet had played little part in the operation so far. Beyond taking command of the second stick, he had made no attempt to encroach on Sebastian's battle plan. He could not, in any case, have played a major role at this stage. Since Sebastian was the only one with knowledge of the target area, it made sense for him to assume leadership of the approach march.

One by one the Guardsmen filed into the helicopters and strapped themselves into their seats. Sebastian was the last to climb aboard. Hat in hand, he found his way to the cockpit and sat down next to the pilot. As soon as the soldiers were in position, the crewman closed the hatch and tapped the pilot on the leg. The rotors were already in motion. The pilot steadily increased the thrust until the Wessex, loaded almost to its limit of 3400 lbs., lurched ponderously into the sky and dipped its beak towards the jungle.

For some time the choppers flew steadily northwards. At one thousand feet, there was little risk of being shot down. Their course took them within a few miles of the ambush area on the starboard side. They continued north for another three miles before the Wessexes began a lazy descent to a sparse clearing at the base of a shallow ridge.

'I'm going to dip below the treeline and hover for a bit,' explained the pilot. 'Anyone watching will think troops are getting out. They'll assume the army is mounting an operation in this area. With luck they'll all head south – right into your arms.'

After thirty seconds the two helicopters rose again in tactical formation and began a broad sweep east and south. To any Warlocks in the vicinity, it must have seemed as if a routine patrol was returning to base.

The pilot consulted the instrument panel and studied his map. Sebastian kept to himself, wishing that this part of the business could be over, yet glad that it wasn't. As the only one who knew where to find the hut, his test was still to come. It would be severe.

'Two minutes to go,' said the pilot at last. 'The hatch won't open until we're below the treeline – I don't want any cowboys having a look at our cargo. You'd better go and join your men now. Hope we meet again. Good luck.'

The red warning light was already on in the cabin. The men were carrying their weapons in their left hands. Like a home-coming pelican the chopper skimmed the treetops and flattened the waving jungle grasses with its downwash. The crewman slid back the hatch. Sebastian caught a glimpse of the ground hurtling beneath the wheels. Then the red light turned green and the deplaning horn burst into sound. With scant ceremony, the crewman pushed him over the edge.

Sebastian landed heavily on both feet, praying to God there were no Warlocks within striking distance. The platoon was helpless while deplaning. He stood beside the hatch and handed down the Guardsmen in rapid succession. Rifles at the high port, they sprinted for the protection of the trees. Once under cover they fanned out swiftly and went to earth, eyes scanning the jungle to their front, searching for the enemy.

Out of the corner of his eye Sebastian saw Malplaquet jump awkwardly from the second chopper and fall to his knees on the ground. He made no move to get up. Behind him, the hatch slammed shut and both helicopters rocketed upwards as if a fire had been lit under them. The crewman gave a cheerful thumbs-up sign. Sebastian returned it weakly and watched him disappear from view. The umbilical cord had been cut. They were in the middle of Warlock country and they were on their own. Operation Pot Luck was under way.

15

The roar of departing engines subsided into the distance, then died altogether. The grass stopped waving. The jungle grew silent once more. Wide-eyed and watchful, the Guardsmen lay prone behind their weapons, raking their arcs of fire for a hint of the enemy. Now was the time for the Warlocks to strike, before the airborne troops had a chance to regroup. Naked and exposed in the open, the soldiers had lost no time burrowing into the undergrowth. They were under cover, hidden from view. All except Malplaquet.

Malplaquet was still on all fours in the middle of the clearing. He had made no attempt to seek the shelter of the trees, but was scratching about in the grass as if searching for something. He seemed unconscious of his surroundings. From where Sebastian was lying, he looked like an elderly gardener pulling up weeds on his allotment.

Sebastian didn't bother to hide his annoyance. At the O group beforehand, he had particularly stressed the importance of keeping out of sight in enemy territory. He had emphasized the need to stay hidden. Yet here was Malplaquet, in full view, rooting around on his hands and knees. It was disloyal.

Sebastian traded glances with Sergeant Ball, who was watching from the shade of a banyan tree. Ball looked sour. He didn't like it either. They waited for perhaps thirty seconds, expecting Malplaquet to join them. Nothing doing. Malplaquet stayed where he was, beyond question looking for something. Sebastian signalled to Ball that he was going out there. Rising cautiously, he sprinted across the open space and skidded down alongside the Company commander.

'What is it?' he hissed. 'What are you trying to find?'

Malplaquet's gaze was bleary. 'My contact lens. From my right eye. It fell out when I hit the ground.'

'You wear contact lenses?' Malplaquet had kept that one a dark secret. Sebastian joined in the hunt and realised at once that it was hopeless. A tiny sliver of transparent plastic would be lost for ever in long grass trampled on by a couple of dozen soldiers. Malplaquet had seen the last of that. Or rather, he hadn't.

'How good is your eyesight?' Sebastian demanded.

'I can't see a blind thing out of the right eye.' Malplaquet was feeling sorry for himself. 'It's not so bad in the left. I can make out most shapes – so long as they're not too far away.'

Silly bugger! What was it Foxtrot had said? Shoot him if he gets out of hand. Sebastian was tempted to put a gun to Malplaquet's head there and then. Instead, taking a grip on him, he half-led, half-dragged him towards the rest of the platoon. Then he joined Sergeant Ball for a whispered conference.

'We'll keep it a secret from the men,' said Sebastian. 'Tell 'em he dropped his watch, if they ask. You'll have to look after him. Stick close behind and make sure he doesn't walk into any trouble.'

'Right,' said Ball. His face, as usual, concealed his outrage. Whatever his private feelings, though, Sebastian knew Ball would keep a firm grip on Malplaquet for the good of the patrol. Sebastian was grateful. Thank God for Ball, and all like him.

Forming up by sections, the platoon fell into line for the three-mile trek to the ambush site. The order of march was single file, Sebastian in front with map and compass; Ball and Malplaquet in the middle; a reliable lance-sergeant at the back, protecting the rear. Partridge was standing immediately behind Sebastian; further back, Turtle and Gilligan took their places in the column. All of them were looking to Sebastian for leadership. All placed their trust in him to shepherd them to the ambush and bring them back alive. Surrounded by thirty heavily-armed and highly professional soldiers, he had never felt more alone.

He had already fixed the bearing on his compass. The course was calculated one degree out of true, so that if he missed the ganja hut at the end of five thousand paces, he would know which way to look for it. He was not confident of finding the hut. Map reading from the air was difficult enough, but at eye level, in a mixture of jungle and swamp, it was next to impossible. To follow a compass needle in a straight line through a belt of mangroves was out of the question. He would just have to do the best he could. And even if his map reading led him to the general vicinity of the hut, he could be within twenty yards of it and never know. The jungle was that thick.

Exuding an assurance he didn't feel, Sebastian signalled the order to advance. The compass led towards a creeper-clad wall of knotted vegetation, half a hundred feet high. It was not practical to cut a path with machetes, because chopped vegetation would mark the passage of troops as efficiently as any signpost. The platoon was supposed to be taking the Warlocks by surprise. They would just have to find a way through it somehow, on hands and knees if necessary, being careful to conceal the evidence of their passing.

For ninety minutes Sebastian followed the anxious needle of the compass, setting as fast a pace as he dared through the undergrowth. He was determined to reach the target before sundown. The route led across a river and through several groves of bamboo. Twice an emissary came forward from Malplaquet ordering the pace to be slowed down. Twice Sebastian ignored the order. With a million dollars waiting at the other end, he realised time was too short to waste.

Shadows lengthened as the sun began to wane. Knowing how quickly night fell in the tropics, Sebastian was on the verge of panic. Ahead, the jungle had given way to a reeking stretch of swamp filled with reeds and green slime. Sebastian moved gingerly towards the edge and looked over to his right. About four hundred yards away, he recognised the overgrown promontory concealing the ganja hut. They were there! One last effort would do it. Exulting inwardly, Sebastian put away the compass. If nothing else, the approach march had been a triumph of map reading, a textbook performance by any standards. So far, so good.

Looking over his shoulder, he caught the eye of the two fan patrol leaders and motioned them forward. They knew what to do. Their job was to fan outwards into the jungle and move ahead of the main body, checking the area for Warlocks. The main body would not advance until the all clear had been given.

An inch before sunset, the fan patrols reported back. Each was positive they had seen nothing. There was no sign of the Warlocks. The place was deserted.

Now came Sebastian's turn. Treading softly, he led the way forward towards the hut, taking care to remain hidden behind the trees. The platoon followed. Sebastian signalled a halt among the mangroves bordering the clearing and stepped into the open on his own to examine the building. Covered by a section of riflemen, he pushed open the hessian curtain and glanced inside. The marijuana was still in place, hidden beneath the mealie cobs. Pollock was still on his pole. No one had been there. The Warlocks had yet to come.

There was just time to set up the ambush before nightfall. Sebastian had already worked out the details. A small track, about eighteen inches wide, led away from the clearing towards the jungle. On the side of the track furthest from the platoon ran a solid wall of foliage. A running man would not slip through this cover in a hurry. It would take him a good ten seconds, and ten seconds was more than enough. He would not escape. On the platoon's side of the track, about twenty yards from it, was the tangle of mangrove trees, thickly embedded in an earthy bank of gnarled roots and twisted trunks. The mangroves supplied camouflage and protection. They also made a good OP for surveillance of the building and the approaches to it.

The killing area would be a twenty-five-yard stretch of open ground straddling the point where the clearing made way for the track. Behind the bank Sebastian placed a fifteen-man killer group – nine riflemen and three machine-gun crews. Taking bushes and trees as aiming marks, he allotted each soldier an arc of fire calculated to saturate the killing ground with crossfire. If it came to a shootout, the Warlocks would be hopelessly outclassed.

A pair of lookouts were concealed thirty yards outwards from each end of the killing ground. Their job was to give warning of the enemy's approach. They did this by pulling a hidden length of wire attached to Sebastian's arm. They were to give it a sharp tug for every Warlock who passed them.

A hundred yards behind the killing ground, the mangroves thinned back to reveal a small patch of open scrub leading down to the swamp. This would have to serve as a base area. Though not ideal, it was good enough for the deposit of back packs and ration boxes. Men off-watch could eat and sleep there. If they made a noise, the sound ought not to carry as far as the track. At one end, Sebastian ordered a shallow latrine to be dug.

It was almost dark now. One last task remained. The marker flares. If the enemy chose to come by night, the killing ground would have to be lit up. Sergeant Ball was the expert here. Leaving Malplaquet anchored to a tree, he joined his platoon commander in the open. Sebastian shook out three RAF ground flares and handed them to Ball, who methodically concealed them in the grass the far side of the path. By day they would be invisible. By night they would illuminate the undergrowth for three long minutes, supplying a garish backdrop for the slaughter in the clearing. Breaking open the top of each flare, Ball inserted a No 33 detonator and connected the leads to the wires of the firing box. Then he took a packet of contraceptives from his pocket and pulled a rubber sheath over each connection to protect it from damp.

Carrying the firing box in his left hand, Sebastian paid out the wire through the undergrowth towards the spot he had selected for a command post. Ball followed, making sure the wire was out of sight. No one would notice it who wasn't expecting to find it.

The command post was in the centre of the ambush. It was occupied by Partridge, the radio operator, and Malplaquet, still sunk in self-pity. His face was red and bleeding from a thorn bush which had lacerated him during the approach march. He had not seen it bent back by the man in front. Since reaching the ambush he had sat hunched beneath a tree, goggling at the blurred shapes around him; in his present condition, he was not even fit to aim a rifle.

Shoot him if he gets out of hand. Well, why not? There was nothing to stop Sebastian. It would be an accident – like the ones the Americans had in Vietnam. It was a straightforward business decision. He could not afford to be soft. He was in command of a dangerous operation, and Malplaquet was a liability to the success of that operation. If the Company Commander got out of hand, Sebastian would shoot him and blame it on the enemy. He wouldn't think twice about it.

No words passed between them, but from his face Sebastian was sure for once that Sergeant Ball was thinking much the same. Ball had been in the army too long to pretend that desperate situations did not require desperate remedies. One peep out of Malplaquet and Ball would be on to him, Sebastian was certain of that. The safety of everyone depended on it.

Sebastian drew Ball aside. He nodded towards Malplaquet. 'You know what to do about him,' he whispered. While not actually tapping the butt of his rifle as he spoke, he did stroke it in a meaningful way, so that Ball would be in no doubt as to the message. Sebastian was scrupulous in his choice of words. Nothing about killing passed his lips. Come the court martial, with Malplaquet lying dead of a bullet in the back, there would be no comeback on Sebastian. No one would be able to accuse him of having given the fatal command. ('But did Mr Clinch actually order you to shoot the deceased?' *Sergeant Ball:* 'Well, no sir, not in so many words'). And there was Foxtrot, too. As a senior officer, it could be argued that he had instructed Sebastian to eliminate Malplaquet, had been responsible for putting the idea into his head. Either way, Sebastian was covered from above and below.

The situation, obviously, was far from satisfactory; but Sebastian told himself in mitigation that the circumstances were exceptional. This was a fighting patrol, prepared at any moment to go into action. At such a time, the machine was only as strong as its weakest link – and the weakest link was unquestionably the Earl of Malplaquet.

Once the bullets began to fly, it made little difference in Sebastian's view whether the one which neutralised the Company Commander belonged to the platoon or to the Warlocks. In Sebastian's view. And in Ball's view too, by the way he acknowledged Sebastian's whisper with a firm nod. It was a business decision, that was all. Something that had to be done.

Unaware of this development, the object of their discussion had roused himself from his despondency and was beginning to give out orders in a low, tremulous voice. The ambush was now in place. In order to maintain it round the clock, schedules would have to be operated to provide rest periods for those not on stag. A roster had been prepared by Sergeant Ball. Malplaquet decided to rearrange it, not because it was inadequate, but because he needed to reassert himself after the débâcle over the contact lens. Under the new scheme, Turtle and two others were scheduled to be asleep at the same time as they were in the firing line. Ball made no comment. He simply nodded encouragement to Malplaquet, then went away and put his own plan into effect.

The night drew in. The men stood to, in their ambush positions. Malplaquet lay on Sebastian's right, about ten yards away, almost in the centre of his line of fire. A shot aimed along the track might without suspicion take off the back of his head. Ball, too, was watching him. One mistake, one stupid dangerous move, and the twelfth Earl of Malplaquet would be zapped with a left and a right before he knew what hit him. On that ominous note, they settled down to wait.

Waiting was the worst part. It needed inexhaustible reserves of mental discipline. Since the slightest movement, the slightest chink of metal on stone, could be enough to alert the enemy, the soldiers were expected to lie still, often as long as ten hours at a stretch. Outside the base area they couldn't eat, scratch or even urinate.

Every night, those not on guard stood awkwardly upright and crept back in the dark, flexing muscles stiff and sore with cramp. Conversation was banned. Meals were eaten cold, in unnatural, ghostly silence. After cleaning their weapons, the men lay down to sleep until they were due for stag. Though the ground was damp and slushy, they fell asleep within minutes. Their last duty before turning in was to urinate along the approaches to the base area, enveloping it in human scent repellent to the animals of the jungle. Most animals took the hint – but not the mosquitoes, sombre blood-sucking creatures which swooped out of the darkness to prey in thousands on their helpless victims.

At daybreak the Guardsmen rose long before first light and queued for the latrine before eating another cold meal. As the days wore on, it became increasingly difficult to go back to reality after a night dreaming of other things. Nobody wanted to return to the ambush. Everybody, Sebastian included, dreaded the rough shaking from Sergeant Ball which heralded the beginning of another marathon.

Morale, however, was excellent. The platoon was thriving on adversity. What had once been an unwieldy collection of the work-shy and truant had suddenly come alive since the beginning of the operation, as if an electric light had been switched on. The soldiers were on their mettle. Now that there was plenty to grumble about, the leading grumblers of the platoon had fallen silent. They were happy, in a curious way. The job had to be done and they were the men to do it. Sebastian was proud of them.

Proud, even, of Turtle. He was a rifleman in the killer group. Oddly enough he had proved a pillar of strength since deplaning from the helicopter. He had lugged a couple of boxes of belt ammunition through the jungle without complaint, and had carried an extra radio on top for good measure. He wasn't allowed to work it, but he was allowed to take the weight. Sebastian had been wrong about him. He was a sound man and a valuable asset to the platoon. It showed, you could never tell. When the going got rough, the most unlikely people came out in front.

Towards evening on the second day, the roster allowed Sebastian two hours' rest in the base area behind the ambush. Sergeant Ball took his place in the killer group. They were careful never to be out of the line together, so that one of them would always be around to bop Malplaquet if he needed it. Sebastian was looking forward to the respite. It would be the first he had had in daylight. Making his way to the rear, he slipped through the discarded equipment and joined the other six Guardsmen also off-duty.

Turtle was among them. He was standing up, enjoying the luxury of stretching his legs, hidden from view by the mangrove trees. A new gold ring adorned his wedding finger. He was still wearing his blue civilian shoes against the day, as far off as ever, that the British military machine disgorged the long-awaited jungle boots. Otherwise, he was properly dressed. From the ankles upwards, he was the same young man who had dominated the screen in Bo Lindström's recent production. Art was the mirror of life. If Lindström had been prepared to wait, he would have been able to film the real thing, instead of a mock ambush. He didn't know what he was missing.

Sebastian sat down next to Turtle and wondered if he dared take off his boots to give his feet an airing. He decided not. It was his experience that nothing ever happened in the army until one took one's boots off – then everything did. It wasn't worth the risk. Instead he took a paperback novel out of his ammunition pouch and settled down for a leisurely read.

War and Peace made an unlikely subject in the middle of an ambush, surrounded by a gang of armed men, but Sebastian needed a change from soldiering to occupy his mind. There was nothing else to do but read. This was a rest period. He did not feel like sleep, and he could hardly go for a walk. It was standard practice for army ambushes of long duration to carry a selection of literature to keep the troops from cracking up. Not usually *War and Peace*, though. Try as he might, Sebastian could not get into it. Somehow the problems of old Russia, of which dress Natasha and Sonja would wear to the ball, failed to engage his attention – probably because he had enough worries of his own, just at the moment. Tolstoy was too heavy for an ambush. Laying him aside, Sebastian looked round to see what the others were reading.

Turtle was the man. He had a fistful of war comics with lurid covers and straight no-nonsense titles to catch the eye. SHEER GUTS, SUICIDE SQUADRON, TARGET FOR TONIGHT. Sebastian picked up SHEER GUTS. It was the story of Jim, a youth of limited intellect, eager to test himself in combat. The narrative was economical.

It was Jim's first taste of battle. He felt cold with fear. Spandaus hammered furiously from the Jerry positions and the acrid smell of cordite stung his nostrils.

Strong as a bull and aching to prove himself as a soldier, Jim was up among the leaders. 'Take that, you dirty Hun!'...

Sebastian read no further. He went back to Natasha.

The more he thought about it, the more the idea of shooting Malplaquet was growing on him. It was an excellent notion. What had begun as a painful necessity was becoming attractive in its own right. Business with pleasure. Chewing it over, Sebastian even managed to persuade himself that the mission could not hope to succeed unless Malplaquet was neutralised. He did not have to be killed. A flesh wound would do – as long as it kept him out of action.

By the end of the third day, after too many hours staring at nothing, too much time brooding to himself, Sebastian was determined to get a shot at Malplaquet. Circumstances demanded it. Above all things, he loved and cherished his platoon. He would not allow their well-being to be jeopardised by the Company Commander's inadequacy. He would shoot Malplaquet first. And maybe kill him.

Malplaquet had no heir. He was a confirmed bachelor. Sebastian would be snuffing out a title that stretched back to 1709, to the War of the Spanish Succession. The first Earl had been a German adventurer and soldier of fortune, a lover of Abigail Hill. Under the Duke of Marlborough, he had commanded a brigade in reserve on the field of Malplaquet. When the Prince of Orange's Dutch troops broke and ran, closely pursued by Louis XIV's army, this unknown outsider plugged the gap and saved the day. To annoy Marlborough, politicians in London thereupon persuaded Queen Anne to elevate him to the English peerage as first Earl of Malplaquet.

Five minutes of confusion on a muddy foreign field, and his descendants had been ruling England ever since. Successive Earls had supported the Tory vote for more than two hundred years. They seldom did more than vote, however. It was a family boast that no Malplaquet had made a speech in the House of Lords since the Capital Punishment Amendment Bill of 1868. The extinction of the line would be no loss to Her Majesty's legislature.

Sebastian cocked an eye in Malplaquet's direction. He was lying on his belly, shoulder against the roots of a tree. A Guardsman lay on either side. Whether Sebastian aimed for the thigh or the head, it would be a difficult, dangerous shot. A one-off job. If he didn't get Malplaquet first time, he wouldn't get him at all. He wasn't going to risk a second attempt.

On the morning of the fourth day it began to rain. Sebastian heard the rain long before he saw it. Far away he heard a thousand Napoleonic drummer boys beating out a dramatic *pas de charge* in menacing echo across the jungle. Nearer and nearer came the noise, louder and louder, until the gloomy sky overhead turned a gloomier grey and the world narrowed into a few square yards of mud and misery. This was tropical rain, stiff and unyielding. Within half a minute the men were soaked beyond redemption. The torrent spared nothing. It thundered down until the swamp rose in flood, seeping forward across the base area and into the latrine pit, which quickly overflowed. Everywhere was rain and wet and filth. Morale, which had been holding up so well, began to crumble – and with it, the resolution to continue.

Why had no one come to pick up the marijuana? Surely the Warlocks should have been there by now? It made no sense to leave all that money lying around unclaimed. Or had the Warlocks seen the helicopters on the first day? Were they playing a double game? Lying low perhaps, not far away, waiting for the patrol to pull out. What was happening?

Strain was beginning to show in the soldiers' faces. Long hours of alertness demanded a price. Tired and disconsolate, the men were losing their edge. Self-discipline had already started to fail, and the platoon no longer believed in Warlocks. They suspected instead an error on somebody's part, a calculation gone wrong. With the downpour came the low point of their efficiency. They lost heart. After the rain, they concentrated only on surviving intact until the business was over – they had abandoned any interest in the outcome.

Sebastian conferred in undertones with Sergeant Ball. They debated whether to call off the ambush. Sebastian was for setting fire to the marijuana and summoning the helicopters to take the platoon away. Ball argued in favour of staying put. To his military mind, a ten-day ambush should last ten days. There was no new information, no evidence that their cover had been blown. They agreed on a compromise. The ambush would remain in position another twenty-four hours. Then, if nothing developed, they would think again.

When the Warlocks did come, no one was ready for them. It was mid-morning on the fifth day. The sun had not yet reached its full power. Sebastian was settling into his niche for another stretch of boredom when the lookout gave a tug on the wire that yanked his elbow from under him.

The man did it again, straight away. Two Warlocks had walked past him and were within thirty yards of the killing ground. Sebastian's mind promptly went blank. He couldn't think what to do. He wondered whether to alert Ball, but decided to remain still. He was paralysed. Hugging the knowledge to himself, he waited for another tug on the wire.

It didn't come. There were only two of them. Sebastian felt the killer group stiffen as the men came into view. Mesmerised, he peered through the foliage at a pair of negroes advancing down the track. They were orthodox Warlocks, long-haired and wild. Both wore American camouflage smocks and carried sub-machine guns on a sling. Their eyes flickered unceasingly back and forth across the jungle, missing little. They meant business.

The men were bang in the middle of the killing area, halfway between the hidden soldiers and the ganja hut. Sebastian was rigid with fright. The platoon outnumbered them fifteen to one, yet it was Sebastian who was scared. He couldn't take his eyes off them.

Horrified, he watched the two Warlocks creep towards the hut. Apparently satisfied that they were alone, one stood guard while the other slipped inside. This was Sebastian's cue. According to the plan, he was to wait until the Warlocks had their hands on the illegal substance before making a move. Then he was to step forward and arrest them. He had rehearsed the formal language: 'I suspect that this article which I have found in your possession is intended to be used for a purpose prejudicial to preservation of the peace.' He would probably be dead before he finished the sentence.

Gripping his rifle, he steadied himself with his other hand and prepared to stand up. He drew his legs forward. The killer group braced themselves expectantly.

Then he felt a third tug on the wire.

They were good, these Warlocks. Somebody had trained them well. The first two were simply scouts for the main body. Their job was to clear the path and spring any surprises, while the rest followed at a safe distance. Even as Sebastian shrank down, the lookout pulled the wire again and again. Three ... four ... five... How many more?

None, as it happened. Five was the limit, all armed, followed by a string of donkeys roped together in close order. The new arrivals made straight for the hut, where the two scouts were dragging out the first of the burlap bags. They had been caught in the act.

'Stay where you are!' yelled Malplaquet, suddenly revealing himself. Sebastian had clean forgotten about him. 'Stand quite still! You're under arrest!'

That broke the spell. Events now happened so fast that everyone told a different story afterwards at the debriefing session. The Warlocks whipped round, took in the situation and scattered for their guns. Trapped square-on to the platoon, Brother Ton Ton opened up with a defiant burst of automatic fire which rattled the trees above their ears. For a second he was firing on his own. Then the platoon joined in. Ton Ton vanished backwards, blasted off his feet. The same exchange killed two donkeys. Across the clearing, the other Warlocks were running for cover. Taken off guard, their shooting was too high. Brother Micah, alone, kept his head. He had almost reached the treeline when he faltered, clutched his leg and slumped to the ground. Crawling painfully, he hobbled on towards the trees. He never made it. He was hit in the stomach and again in the chest, and fell dead across the path.

The Warlocks had disappeared. One of them, shot in the thigh, lay in the grass with his arms above his head in token of surrender. The others had reached the undergrowth. They did not get far. The machine guns came after them, clattering across the foliage in a long sweeping arc that sliced through trees and made short work of human flesh. Sebastian let the guns have their way for a while, then yelled for a ceasefire. There was nothing more to be done. The action was over. It had lasted twenty seconds.

At first the clearing was silent. Then, from behind the foliage, a ragged white singlet appeared on the end of a rifle. The survivors wished to surrender. Stricken with shock, they emerged from their hiding place, cautiously at first, then with gathering urgency as they hastened to give themselves up. There were three of them, one seriously wounded in the back. Added to those in the clearing, that made two killed, four taken prisoner and one who had got away. He was never seen again.

Malplaquet took charge of the captives. They were close enough for him to see them with his good eye. The man wounded in the back could not talk. He lay moaning on the ground while Gilligan searched through his clothes. Gilligan made a bad job of it. His hands shook and he was trembling all over, letting go of the tension which gripped his body. Sebastian was trembling too. He had never been under direct fire before. The jolt to his system was absolute. His limbs were in open rebellion – it was a full hour before he regained control.

A single shot broke the silence as Sergeant Ball lifted his rifle to the head of a donkey mutilated in the crossfire. The animal's hindquarters lay feebly on the ground, its entrails spilling over the earth. Its head was twisted towards the sky, unnaturally upright, tethered to the donkey in front. This sight moved Sebastian more than anything. For the two dead men, sprawled in the dirt, he had no feeling. Not hate, not pity. Yet for the donkey, suffering without knowing the reason why, he felt strong remorse. He wanted to weep.

The Warlock wounded in the thigh was sitting up in the grass, tended by Partridge. The wound was not serious. A field dressing had already stopped the bleeding. Sebastian looked up from the man's thigh to his face, framed in braided ringlets, and recognised him immediately from his photograph as Leon Sullivan, leader of the Gris Gris movement. He knew, too, where he had seen him before.

'Sullivan,' he said.

'Clinch.'

Sullivan had looked very different then. His hair had been much shorter and he had been clean-shaven. Sebastian's mind went back over the years to a fine day in autumn, the first day of his military career. To the clothing store, Agincourt Company, Mons Officer Cadet School. They were issuing uniforms. At the head of the queue, a black man had come out of the store with a bundle of equipment balanced expertly on his head. This black man.

'I know you. You were at Mons. You won the prize for best coon.' ('And the award for the most outstanding overseas cadet goes to junior under-officer L. StJ. Sullivan of the Casuarina Defence Force.' Applause from spectators at the commissioning parade.)

'I know you, too. You had the bed next to Baraza. Remember him?'

Sebastian remembered Baraza all right. Big Black Baraza. He had been the terror of nuns for miles around Aldershot. Sebastian had been delegated to help him with his alphabet during the early, difficult weeks of training.

'He's doing very well for himself now,' he said. 'He's Minister of Fiscal Development in Uganda.'

This was absurd. Swapping reminiscences with a common criminal. An old Agincourt man, and now a criminal. A renegade, trained by the British, biting the hand that fed him. No wonder the Warlocks had been so efficient.

'You'd better tell me about it,' said Sebastian. He could guess much of the story. 'I suppose you resigned your commission as soon as you got home and set up on your own?'

Sullivan grinned. He was not embarrassed. 'Of course! A good military education is too valuable to waste on soldiering. I never went back at all. I went straight over to Santa Monica and got them to supply me with all the ammunition and small arms I needed. The market for small arms is tremendous. Very buoyant – as long as you know where to sell them. The Santa Monicans thought I was fomenting revolution. So did the brothers who bought the stuff.'

'And the ganja?'

'A sideline, old boy. That's how it began, anyway. I was smuggling rifles across the river and it seemed a shame not to try my luck with ganja as well. The brothers thrive on it. And the surplus sells for a fortune on the open market. A thousand dollars a kilo. You wouldn't believe it!'

'How about the Gris Gris movement, then? That nonsense about spirits and witchcraft?'

'A pose, nothing more. The brothers are all believers. I had to go along with them. It was the only way to keep them loyal.'

He was clever, no doubt about that. The most outstanding overseas cadet. Once Casuarina became independent, he would certainly find a place in the Cabinet.

Sebastian turned away. He had seen all he wanted of Leon Sullivan. He hadn't known him at Mons. They had been in different platoons and had worked with different instructors. The platoons didn't mingle much – it was part of the system. Sullivan had been just another face among the mass of Commonwealth cadets. He must have appeared somewhere in the group commissioning photograph – on the front row, probably, among the directing staff, dressed in Sam Browne belt and sword. But he had made no impression on

Sebastian. Until now, Sebastian couldn't even remember what he looked like.

Operation Pot Luck was all wrapped up. Lord Malplaquet congratulated himself on a job well done – he didn't realise the peril he had been in. Picking up the radio handset, he put through a message to Battle Group Blenheim. His voice was full and confident. 'Little Plum,' he announced. 'Little Plum.' It was the signal for successful completion of the operation. The duty signalman at Battle Group would alert Foxtrot, who in turn would call for the helicopters to come and collect the patrol. There would be three this time, to take care of the dead and wounded and the bulk of the marijuana. They would not land at the hut, but were scheduled to zero in on a meadow about six hundred yards away, where the obstruction angle for take-off was less hazardous.

Now that the ambush was over, the ban on speech had been lifted. The men were free to talk. After five days' enforced silence, their tongues ran away with them. They all spoke at once, nobody listened, and the jungle filled with shouts and laughter, pitched a shade too high. The escape of pressure was almost audible. Tramping cheerfully through the undergrowth, the men went to collect their back packs and equipment from the muddy base area. The look-outs scrambled to their feet and the outlying sentries were called in. Sebastian undertook the task of removing Pollock's head from its pole. He wrapped it gingerly in a bandage for interment at a later date. Carrying their kit, the men returned from the base area. They formed up under Sergeant Ball on the path leading towards the helicopter meadow.

Ball took a roll call. The Guardsmen numbered off by sections. Ammunition and casualty states were reported. Ammunition was still in good supply and nobody had been wounded. But one soldier was missing. Turtle.

'He must have got lost in the ulu somewhere,' Ball reported to Sebastian. 'I'll go and collect him.'

'If you would, please, Sarnt Ball. And tell him to hurry. The choppers won't wait.'

Turtle was lying on his back in the ambush area, half-hidden behind a bush. His body was motionless and quiet. A Warlock bullet had passed through his neck, killing him instantly. No one had seen him die.

Sebastian gave orders for his body to be rolled into a groundsheet and carried to the landing site. The incoming helicopters would bring body bags for the dead. Sebastian cut the identity discs from the string around Turtle's neck and stuffed them into his pocket, together with a rain-soaked comic he found in the grass nearby. It seemed the least he could do.

The march to the landing ground was subdued and silent. No one wanted to speak. On reaching the meadow, Sebastian told the Guardsmen to fan out clockwise and watch the jungle to their front until the transport arrived. This precaution was more for show than anything. They needed something to keep their minds occupied. While the men went to ground, Sebastian took out a smoke grenade and prepared it for firing. The smoke would indicate wind direction for the helicopters. He tested the wind with his finger. It was blowing from the west. He walked across the clearing and placed the canister at the down-wind edge of the landing site, ready for the sound of the aero-engines. Then he sat down and cried.

16

The legions depart, the regiment goes home.

Already the advance party of the incoming battalion had arrived from Britain. Strange pale Scotsmen in kilts and green shirts, professional Highlanders, occupied the airport and had taken possession of the bridge leading to Santa Monica. The last platoon of Guardsmen had been withdrawn from the frontier. In celebration of this event, a lone fife player of the Gobelin Guards had marched by himself through the streets of Mango Creek, to be followed, a few days later, by the bagpipes of the Jocks playing a selection of laments.

Number 9 Platoon was now resident at Fort Pitt, counting the hours to departure. The men were kept busy all day, cleaning, painting and scrubbing, checking stores and making up deficiencies for the handover to the new arrivals. The Gobelin lines would be delivered in spotless condition. Orderly room, pioneer shop and corporals' mess; MT section, guardroom and NAAFI block; every building was swept and spruced and polished until no trace remained of its previous occupants.

After the arrest of Leon Sullivan the Gris Gris rebellion, if rebellion it was, had come to an end. Deprived of leadership, purged of their criminal element, the Warlocks had simply faded away, back into the obscurity from which they had sprung. To be sure, they still smoked ganja and dreamed of Africa, but they no longer posed a threat to the government. Without Sullivan to direct them, the majority had thrown away their weapons and returned to their homes. A few went rogue and continued to roam the jungle, criminals still, object of sporadic sorties by British and French troops. But most reverted to civilisation, lured by an unofficial amnesty and a vigorous hearts and minds campaign, mounted by the army, aimed at rehabilitation rather than retribution. The campaign was a success. In the course of time the Warlocks not only learned to live with imperialism but became a popular cult in their own right, attended by a considerable following. Their long hair and curious ways made them a firm hit with tourists. The days of Sullivan's influence were over. His name had been forgotten. He was in prison and there, until the territory received its independence, he would stay.

Of Turtle, no one had spoken. No one wanted to know. His body lay in a metal coffin, waiting for the flight to England. There it would be taken to Wolverhampton in accordance with his mother's wishes. The funeral was to be a military one. A guard of honour from Chelsea Barracks was already rehearsing the drill. Sebastian was planning to attend, and so were most of the men in the platoon.

Adelita, the widow Turtle, had first been shocked, then angry, then defiant when Sebastian broke the news to her. She shed no tears. Instead, after a pause for reflection, she married again. True love blossomed often in her garden. Within a few days of Turtle's death she entered the state of matrimony for a second time – and her husband once again was a member of 9 Platoon, Partridge.

Sebastian did not find out about it until afterwards. Partridge came alone to tell him. He was sheepish. He did not seek to justify his action. 'It seemed a good idea, sir,' was all he could bring himself to say.

British soldiers were extraordinary. Sebastian had always thought he understood Partridge; yet this was beyond belief. Later he discovered that it was part of a broader phenomenon which had swept through the ranks on the eve of the battalion's return home. Soldiers everywhere were falling over themselves to get married. Platoon commanders reported that in most cases the Guardsmen were hooking up with girls they hardly knew, still less cared about. The idea of a wedding was the thing. Some deep romantic chord in the soldiers' nature impelled them to go back to England with a bride, a native girl from the tropics, whose life would henceforth be transformed. Partridge was far from being the only one. There were plenty like him, who got married in a rush and never knew why they did.

Not everyone followed his example, however. Many Guardsmen chose the opposite course. For every local girl who married a British soldier, there were half a dozen forming an indignant queue outside the orderly room, waiting for the Commanding Officer to hear their petitions for breach of promise. Tales of duplicity were common to all. Some girls had been deceived by several different soldiers. Some soldiers had deceived several different girls. The Commanding Officer listened to each case in turn, while pregnant females on one hand demanded passage to England and amnesic Guardsmen on the other denied all knowledge, carnal or otherwise, of the matter under discussion. The Commanding Officer judged harshly, but with discretion. No marriage certificate, no flight. There was nothing else he could do.

The day of departure arrived. The transport plane earmarked for 9 Platoon had appeared with the dawn and had been three hours on the ground. It came from England and had earlier deposited a company of blinking, owlish Jocks into the sunlight. In their place the Colours of the Gobelin Guards were piped aboard, together with a flag-draped coffin bearing Turtle's body. The Guardsmen followed silently behind. In single file they ascended the ramp and were directed to their seats. There was no ceremony, no poignant leave-taking. The country had gone sour on 9 Platoon. It no longer held any charm for them. They wanted only to get away.

Carrying her daughter and a hat box, Adelita was sitting with the platoon at the rear of the aircraft. She had two husbands on board, one in the seat beside her, the other grey and stiff, shrouded from view behind a mound of equipment. This was her first flight. Shrill with excitement, she gesticulated through the window to the crowd of bystanders, Mme Boongay among them, who had come to say farewell. An assembly of jilted women had also gathered, arms folded, in the lee of the control tower. Some carried suitcases and were hoping for a last-minute change of heart. Others had become angry. Most nursed the beginnings of a bulge in the belly. Like the animals who arrived too late for the Ark, they looked on with a mixture of yearning and betrayal as the aircraft's tail ramp slammed shut. In a few months, the first of them would give birth to a crop of woolly-headed half-castes, children of the regiment, waifs who would never know their fathers – if, indeed, their mothers ever had.

Après la guerre fini,
Tous les soldats partis,
Mademoiselle avec piccanini,
Souvenir des Anglais.

Engines at full power, the aircraft began to pick up speed. The irate knot of women receded swiftly down the runway – first a blur, then a speck, then simply a memory as the plane lumbered into the sky. Goodbye girls, goodbye Casuarina. Next stop Nairobi. Then Cyprus and the Mediterranean. The battalion was posted home, with no regrets. Never had a movement order been more welcome.

Sebastian unfastened his seat belt and lay back. Underneath his seat, he stowed a new pair of boots. Jungle boots, size thirteen. They were addressed to Guardsman Turtle. They had arrived on the plane that was bringing him home.

A cheer, spontaneous and heartfelt, went up as the aircraft touched down in Oxfordshire. It was followed by an outburst of applause. All ranks were glad to be back and made no bones about it. Despite the rhetoric of the recruiting posters, a tropical clime offered no substitute for the cold grey murk of England in December.

Beyond the Customs barrier, a fleet of coaches stood waiting to transport the battalion to London. The countryside was gloomy and bleak. For Adelita Partridge, wearing only a thin print dress, the chill wind across the plain was an unwelcome revelation, the first pinprick of doubt in her frowning, petulant face. For everyone else, it was home.

The journey to Chelsea Barracks lasted almost two hours along wide, straight roads of miraculous metal, no potholes, no river drifts, no mud, no dust. There were neat little houses beside the road, with trim ordered gardens and well-kept hedges. Roundabouts with lawns; green fields and pony clubs. Windsor Castle in the distance, and the roof of Eton College chapel. Runnymede, the Kennedy memorial, and the outer suburbs of London. Then the inner city, approached from the west, the tall stucco buildings, the boutiques and bistros of the King's Road. Civilisation! It seemed another age since Sebastian had led the outward-bound convoy down that same road. The women were dressed differently from six months ago. Their heels were much higher, their clothes more bizarre. As before, they took no notice of the sunburned soldiers who gaped at them from the coach windows. They didn't know the battalion had been away. They didn't know Turtle was dead. They didn't care.

Chelsea Barracks now. Sentry on the gate, grinning all over his face. Travel warrants and a leave pass made out for four weeks. Then home. Goodbyes at the guardroom, rushing to catch a train. Partridge shook hands with Sebastian. He was going north to introduce his wife and step-daughter to Nottingham. Sergeant Ball, by contrast, was going nowhere. He lived in married quarters, and Mrs Ball was already on at him to do something about the plumbing. A few soldiers were spending the first seven days of their leave at the army's VD hospital, for observation and treatment. The married among them had lied to their wives about their home-coming date. Others were being posted away from the battalion. The Intelligence Officer, for example. Having failed his A Level, Foxtrot had given up his legal ambitions and signed on for another three years with the Colours. He had been promoted to major and was already packing a bag for Staff College.

Malplaquet, also, was assured of his future in the army. His command of the battalion had been announced in the rank of Lieutenant Colonel. He had a medal, too. He was Lt. Col. the Earl of Malplaquet, MC. He had been awarded the Military Cross for his performance in the swamp:

Although incapacitated at an early stage, he nonetheless led the men across difficult terrain towards their objective. At the moment of contact with the enemy, he displayed exemplary courage and devotion to duty, killing two of the enemy and capturing four. His personal conduct and disregard for danger inspired everyone under his command. By his gallant action, the Casuarina campaign was brought to a successful conclusion.

Nothing for Turtle. His death was an embarrassment. Not even a mention in the papers, because Willie Hogan, new owner of a Ford Capri, had been recalled to Fleet Street before the final confrontation with the Warlocks. Bo Lindström's film was Turtle's only epitaph. In two days Sebastian would travel to the Midlands for the funeral. He would meet Turtle's mother and attempt to explain how her only son had died. Meantime, however, he had an evening to himself in London, the first long-awaited night of leave. He had been planning it for months. He was going out to dinner in Piccadilly, right in the heart of London. He was going to spend the evening in a restaurant at a corner table, doing nothing in particular, just looking at the clothes and the people and listening to them talk. Enjoying the peace and watching the world go by. Remembering it all.

Sebastian changed into a pinstripe suit and Brigade of Guards tie. The suit was loose around his waist and smelled of must. The barrack guard saluted as he stepped into the street. At the corner of the King's Road he caught a taxi and asked to be put down outside St James's Palace. The journey took ten minutes.

A Gobelin Guardsman, one of the rear party, was doing a two-hour stint at the entry to St James's. He was standing in front of his sentry-box, surrounded by an unseasonal group of American tourists. The group's overnight bags proclaimed their place of origin as Terre Haute, Indiana. One of them, a middle-aged man in a baseball cap, was more knowledgeable than the rest. He had established himself as the party's military authority.

'Chocolate soldiers,' he told the others derisively, pointing to the sentry. 'They never fight.' He shook his head. 'They only stand on guard.'

Printed in Great Britain
by Amazon

51906319R00103